DIRTY WILD SULTAN

ALLURING RULERS OF AZMIA
BOOK ONE

MAHI MISTRY

Dirty Wild Sultan

Copyright © 2021 Mahi Mistry

Published by Mahi Mistry
Cover Design by German Creative
Edited by Creech Enterprise
Proofread by Sisters Get Lit.erary Author Services
ISBN e-Book: 978-93-5426-547-1
ISBN paperback: 978-93-5457-909-7

I would split open my heart
with a knife, place you
within and seal my wound,
that you might dwell there
and never inhabit another
until the resurrection and
judgment day—thus you
would stay in my heart
while I lived, and at my death
you too would die in the
entrails of my core, in
the shadow of my tomb.

— IBN HAZM

Dedicated to the one who inspired it
and will never read it

PART I

"Because, Princess Nasrin,
I am asking you to marry me."

1

ZAIN

I didn't deserve to be the Sultan of Azmia.

The thought rang hollow against my entire body. Pounding in my head increasing when people on the floor kept laughing and talking, dancing in-tune with the sounds of gentle instruments played by the musicians. Walls of the Court Room felt like they were getting smaller and smaller as each minute passed by. Shrinking down on the dais where I sat, on the throne that I didn't deserve to be seated on.

Its dark color leeched of any life. Black against the beige mosaic of the Court Room, the dome at the center glowing brightly as foreign royals awed at the structure. Awed at me, the sheathed sword leaning on the lion's leg of the throne.

My legs tensed, my neck straining after nodding at the guests who had arrived at my palace, my entire body locking and coiling—

"Stop glaring at everyone, Brother," Khalid drawled, prowling towards the obsidian throne. I gave him a look—a look to *behave* himself—when he left two twin princesses of our neighboring country on the floor and placed himself on the arm of the throne. "These princesses are here for your attention, and you are doing your best to scare them away. Here."

I unclenched my jaw and looked at him, his face so similar to mine. Dark slashing brows, sharp cheekbones and eyes the color of dark chocolate. They held more pain than I could ever imagine in my thirty-three years of life.

"I do not want to indulge myself with any alcohol, Khalid. You are already reeking of it," I said, glancing at the crowd. The mothers with their young daughters fawning at us, wishing their daughter would grab the attention of either me, Sultan of Azmia or my brother, Prince of Azmia.

"Why do I need to look for a bride when this party is held for Zara's birthday?" I grumbled to myself, making Khalid chuckle.

We held the party for my sister, the only Princess of Azmia, Zara Al Latif, who would turn nineteen when the clock struck midnight. We were celebrating her birthday and also welcoming the New Year. Zara was born on New Year's Day, and I and Khalid were both relieved and sad that we would celebrate her birthday in a few hours. Relieved that she would be more independent, responsible; and sad that we wouldn't be able to make sure she was safe with… *men*, boys of her age, when she was away for her studies.

Khalid pressed an intricate golden cup in my hand, the auburn liquid swishing in it. "Drink this. It will make you feel more relaxed and… if you are lucky, you will finally get laid, Zain."

I glared at him when he smirked at me, sauntering away to find the twin princesses and warm their bed for the night. Blood rushed to my cheeks. I gulped the burning liquid down my throat, relishing the scorching taste it left on my lips.

Unfortunately for me, my younger brother knew I had

never slept with anyone… had sex with anyone. I was a virgin. A thirty-three-year-old, Sultan of the most powerful country in the Middle East, was a virgin. I planned to keep it that way. I did not mind that one bit. I was perfectly fine pouring my energy into ruling the country, being a better Sultan than my father ever was and taking care of my siblings as the oldest.

Even though it came to using my own hands during unfortunate events, I did not see the need to seek any female for… more pleasure.

"Found anyone yet?" Zara, my little sister, asked, lacing her arm around my elbow when I walked down the steps from the dais to the marble floor designed in beautiful, tangled patterns.

It was not my idea to keep the throne and Court Room but our advisor, Rahim, felt the need to keep it as it was over a hundred years old.

"No luck, yet," I replied, thanking her for sticking to my side and not letting me walk alone among the women who kept eyeing me.

Just like the unnecessary throne that we didn't want or need, our advisor wanted me, the Sultan of Azmia, the Golden Country, to get married and have heirs. I had scoffed at that notion when I was twenty-five, but almost a decade later I could not scoff and ignore it anymore. To protect my country and be a better sultan, I knew the day would come where I would have to find a woman to get married and have heirs.

Even though I wanted to stay celibate and not have any children of my own. I had decided that fifteen years ago.

Her beautiful chestnut wavy hair gleamed in the light when she asked, "Can I go with Khalid to our club?"

I looked at her innocent elfish face, her hazel eyes similar to mine and Khalid's, but the difference of her pale skin to our tan-golden skin was noticeable. She was the daughter of our second mother, who married our father when he visited London nineteen-years ago.

"You know I won't allow you to go to the club. You are—"

"Too young?" she asked. The beauty spot above her lip shifted when she narrowed her eyes at me. *Uh-oh*, she was angry. But it didn't matter, Khalid was the fun brother for her and I was the *less*-fun brother. "Khalid will be there, Zain. You can't always say no to me. I will be nineteen in a few hours, for fuck's sake!"

"Language, Zara!" I said. "Khalid won't be able to keep an eye on you the entire night, and you are the only Princess of Azmia, you know how precious you are."

She gave me a deadpanned look and pointed towards her two bodyguards, who were a foot away from us. I hired them for her protection, and even though there were guards stationed everywhere in the palace, those two were for her own safety.

Before I could speak, Rahim, our advisor, walked towards us, clearing his throat. He was dressed in a beige cotton tunic and pants, an upgrade from the usual white clothes he wore. He bowed his head, wishing Zara a happy birthday who hugged him in return, complimenting the new tunic.

I hid my smile, watching them together. Rahim was less of our advisor and more of a parental figure for all of us. He had taken the role well after what happened with our father. His voice was raspy when he said, "The Sultan of Al Naaem wants to speak with you."

"Not now, Rahim," I said, pointing towards Zara, who was humming to herself and avoiding the eyes of young princes her age.

Talking to my sister and making her feel heard was my main priority—

"He has two daughters that would like to meet you, Sultan," he emphasized.

I took a deep breath and pinched the bridge of my nose. Looking at Zara's wide hazel eyes, begging me to allow her to go. It was enough for me to say *yes*. She grinned, a dimple poking her cheek as she hugged me.

"Thank you, thank you, thank you!" Zara giggled, the sound making my heart light. "You are the best brother ever!"

"Don't let Khalid hear that," I chuckled, hugging her back. "And don't make me regret my decision, Zara. You know what you mean to this country, to us. Don't let any stupid boy break your heart."

With the sheer excitement sparkling in her eyes, it must be a miracle she would have heard me. She was already running away to get dressed for the club; her smile wide. I watched her dark hair as she disappeared from the crowd.

My head took me back to the dark place.

♚

THE SOUNDS OF OUR FEET RUNNING DOWN THE COOL MARBLE floors echoed in the silent night. The only other noise we heard was her cries. Zara's cries.

"If he hurts her—" Khalid swore, following me.

"I won't let that happen," I promised my nineteen-year-old brother. His short hair flopping on his forehead as the guards stopped us outside the Sultan's room. They shook their heads, their eyes cold.

"If you don't open this door, I will make sure your family pays for it," I lied, clenching my fists as I threatened his family. Their eyes widened, Khalid swallowing when we heard another cry from our six-year-old sister.

Rahim, the advisor, called off the guards towards him, nodding at us as we entered the room. Our hearts in our throats. There… Salman Al Latif, our father, holding the dainty wrist of—

"Khalid, Zain… I want to leave," Zara cried, her eyes red and swollen as tears slid down her flushed cheeks. Her hair was rumpled, just like her night pajamas. Moments ago, we had been in her room, watching a Disney movie and Khalid reading her a book.

But now, our father was forcing her to accept the proposal of a betrothal when at her age her only worry should be to learn and play.

"*Baba!*" Khalid yelled, "Stop it. You are hurting her."

It had been a mess after that. A mess of shouts, cries and blood. So much blood that it had stained the tunics Khalid and I wore. The splatter of blood covering Zara's cheeks and neck, another splatter on the empty wall of our father's room as he died in front of our eyes.

♛

"Sultan!"

I snapped back to reality, turning my head to Rahim, who tilted his head at me. *Right*. That happened years ago. There was no need for me to worry about it.

Facing Zara's guards, I ordered, "Keep your eyes on her drink the entire time and double the surrounding protection." I made sure Khalid knew she would be at the club. Even though it was our club, I wanted to make sure nothing happened to her. Especially when she would turn nineteen in a few hours.

I faced the advisor, his wise face wrinkled with old age, his eyes shining with wisdom. I leaned forward with my arm, "Lead me to meet the princesses, Rahim."

The walk to my study was silent, the night stars twinkling brightly as the wind whispered through the pillars.

There were fireworks to celebrate my sister's birthday, making the corners of my lips curl. It was said that the Golden Palace of Azmia took a hundred years to complete. My late father made sure that no one dared to infiltrate the palace even though no country would be stupid enough to go against us.

Rahim walked beside me in the ancient hallways of the palace, lit by golden chandeliers over the domes, making the intricate designs glow. "If this engagement succeeds, it would benefit both Azmia and Al Naaem and the future generations."

That was all I needed to know. I could get married to either of the princesses if they would have me as their husband. But the marriage would only succeed on my terms if my partner agreed not to have sex with me. They could have secret lovers of their own for all I cared, in their privacy. But I would never engage in any sexual activities, for that matter.

Even with my own future wife.

I had seen how my father treated my mothers and how he raised Khalid and me with his cruelty. We still bore his marks of anger. I did not wish to have any child of my own and behave worse than my father.

Especially when that night was stuck in my head like a nightmare turned reality, rolling over and over and watching my siblings di—

"What is troubling you?" Rahim asked, his weathered face concerned.

"That night." I took a deep breath, "I was thinking about the night he died."

"If the ghosts of the past are bothering you, it is better to leave them be." He laid his hand on my shoulder, giving me a brief smile. "Focus on the present, child."

I watched him walk ahead of me, the guards waiting

behind me as I pondered over his response. Leave Rahim to make me feel like a five-year-old having an existential crisis.

Shaking off the events of that night, I squared my shoulders. The guards opened the mahogany doors to the private study room. I had only one thing in mind.

If the sexless marriage would benefit Azmia and my family, I would do *anything*.

♛

"So, what plans do you have for your future?" I asked, clearing my throat at the stunning olive-skinned twin princesses. The only way I could tell the difference between them was how they had chosen different colored dresses. Blue and green, which made their skin glow.

Rahim had forgotten to mention that they were the same twin princesses that Khalid was flirting with a few moments ago. Their father had greeted me and left the room with my advisor and the guards, leaving me alone to engage and talk with them.

They shared a mischievous look and giggled. "We have no plans, Sultan Zain," the princess in blue purred. "We would enjoy whatever you offer us."

I sighed in relief, relaxing back in the comfortable chair. I could offer them a sexless and loveless marriage and—

"Anything you want to offer us, Sultan," the princess in the green dress whispered, standing up, walking towards me with a gleam in her dark eyes.

Wait…

"What the hell are you doing?" I asked, quickly turning my head when she unclasped the hooks of her top, removing it and baring herself in front of me.

I took a deep breath, squeezing my eyes shut and stopping myself before I could threaten their entire lineage for having the audacity to be so… *argh, fuck.*

"Please cover yourself. I do not want to—"

"Look at us, Sultan Zain," her twin said. "We are here for your pleasure."

Grumbling under my breath, I leaned back as far as I could when I felt their hands on me, gliding over my legs and stroking my face. I pulled them off and stood up, walking away from them and focusing my attention on my breath.

If I order to get them executed, I will be at war with Al Naeem. Which is the last thing I want right now.

But I didn't hold back the anger in my voice. "If you do not cover yourself in ten seconds, I will make sure you and your family never enter my palace again. Let alone my country."

"But Sultan—"

"I am not interested in… whatever you are thinking about." My cheeks heated with blood.

I heard some shuffling and turned around when they told me they were decent. They both eyed me warily. "Are you into men?"

I sighed. If I had a penny for each time someone asked me that, I would be three pennies richer than I was, which was not much, but it counted. "No, I am not, and even if I was, it won't be any of your concern," I said in my stern voice. Their demeanor changed when they realized I was truly angry with them. "Now explain to me, why did you *both* feel the need to do what you just did?"

"To seduce you and hopefully be the future Sultana."

I eyed them. "Both of you?"

They shrugged. "Many sultans have over one wife."

I rubbed a hand down my face. "Not me. I prefer monogamous relationships." Ignoring their cooing, I added, "You don't need to do that to seduce anyone, do you hear me? If they can't sit and talk to you for five minutes without you having to strip your clothes, then for fuck's sake, *don't marry them.* You both are princesses of Al Naeem. Our countries fought side by side a hundred years ago."

They looked down at their laps and murmured a quick apology. The princess in blue said, "We were warned you might behave this way, Sultan. It was our fault that we wanted to try to seduce you. I assure you—*we* assure you we won't bother you again."

I nodded, stopping them to ask, "Who warned you?"

They stopped at the door. The princess in the green dress smiled at me, "Prince Khalid."

That *motherfucker.*

2

NASRIN

I held my breath when the smoke of the hookah flew past me, the old Sheikh and my father, Hamid Elbaz, who was the old Sultan of Maahnoor, laughing together.

The stench of the old smoke overpowered the musky jasmine perfume I had donned moments ago. I wanted to leave. My body coiling tightly, my spine straight and tense, I felt sick. Swallowing, I tried to control the bile in my throat that was threatening to pour out.

Seeing what I had for lunch would hopefully make him disgusted enough to take back his offer of proposal.

"How old did you say she is again?" The old Sheikh hoarsely asked, coughing as he rested his palm on his belly. His two wives were seated beside him, a veil covering their faces as they sat frozen.

I pitied them. I truly did. Because if my father dared to accept the proposal of the Sheikh, I would do anything to not end up like them.

"I am twenty-six," I said, meeting his stare and not daring

to look away even when his eyes glazed, looking at me. My body.

Sheikh grumbled, "That's not too young, is it? But she looks old enough to be my daughter, so that's—"

Imran Elbaz, my younger brother, cleared his throat, gaining his attention. I sighed in relief when he asked him a question regarding his city. Sadiq Elbaz, my eldest brother and the current Sultan of Maahnoor, shook his head at us, his eyes sharp and cold.

I looked away, feeling helpless and sad. I hated the feeling. I wished my mother were with me, holding my hand and telling my father to reject the Sheikh's offer. That I deserved better than the sixty-something old sheikh who was only interested in my body. But cancer had taken her away from me when I was nine. She would never be back.

A small part of my cheerful brothers left with her, and the father who used to smile at me, who'd bring me a jasmine flower every morning.

It took her so far that I was alone in the palace that was supposed to be my home, but never felt like it. My sanctuary, surrounded by the people who didn't feel like my family anymore. I missed my brothers, my father, and especially my mother.

"I would need to talk to my daughter before we accept the proposal," my father said, giving me a forced smile, but I won't meet his eyes. He knew I would rather rot than marry the Sheikh.

"I have heard she has rejected every proposal for marriage," the old Sheikh replied, scoffing at me. "So proud at her age, don't you think?"

I wondered how sharp the edge of the fruit knife was. How would it feel to hear him squeal with fear if I held it against his neck?

Clenching my hands, I thought about my mother, my

master's degree that was laying on my dresser, my future of working with animals and helping them.

"I am not accepting your marriage proposal." Standing up, I stared down at the Sheikh, his guards taking a step closer. "I have heard that you still take dowries from your wife's family. That is illegal, isn't it?" I enjoyed the way color leached from his face. I smiled. "Don't make me file a complaint towards you to the council, Sheikh. I have heard that they publicly execute the people who still follow that practice."

"Nasrin Elba—"

My father's shout was muffled as I grinned, walking out of the study, my body lighter than before, my muscles relaxing. The citrus scent was tinged in the air, sunlight streaming through the dusky pillars of the old palace. I wished my father or brother would take better care of it. The paint was fading and the once beautiful intricate designs were getting covered in dust.

Sighing, I made my way to my room, the simple white-washed walls, curtains, dresser and a four-poster bed. I missed my dorm room from university. It had more liveliness to it than the boring room I had grown up in.

"You should have at least tried to accept his proposal, Nasrin."

I rolled my eyes when Sadiq followed me. "I will say the same thing when an old queen asks for your hand in marriage, Sadiq."

"He is not that old."

I turned around and gave him a look. His aquiline nose flared, his cheekbones high, similar to mine. Even our golden-brown eyes were the same. I hated how many similarities we had because it reminded me of our mother.

"If you would marry him, then Maahnoor can import better vegetables and fruits from his city," he said, following me in my room, watching me remove the jewelry.

"If you wanted that to happen, Sadiq," I said. "Then you should try harder to be a better Sultan."

Silence fell in the room, and I knew I might have crossed a line, but I wouldn't back down from stating the truth. He had been crowned as sultan five years ago and our country had made no progress or development as it needed.

"You should think before you speak, Nasrin. You are talking to the Sultan of Maahnoor and as a sultan, I can order you to marry him," he threatened, his face turning sharp and angry.

My heart hammered in my ears as I looked at him. "I know I buried you with my mother, Sadiq." He took a sharp breath, his eyes wide as he stared at me.

The door of my room opened and Imran stormed in. "Stop, both of you. Sadiq, we both know we will find a way to import better food to Maahnoor in some way or another. But it won't happen by selling our sister to that old reek. Not when I am still alive."

I held my breath when they stared down at each other. Despite being three years younger than me, they both had the same height. I loved Imran more than Sadiq, but it didn't mean I wanted them to fight for me. Especially when I had already rejected that sheikh.

"Sadiq, please leave my room. I don't want to clean either of your blood from my freshly washed sheets," I said, crossing my arms.

Sadiq looked at me, his jaw clenched as he walked out of my room, bumping his shoulder against Imran. We both sighed when he left the room.

"I am sorry for what happened, Nasrin," Imran whispered when I loosened my hair from the braid, running my hand through the dark hair.

"What do you mean? You have nothing to apologize for."

"I know, but I wish I could help you. I know you don't want to get married yet, Father and Sadiq keep pestering you for it," he said, his voice soft.

My heart ached hearing him. I chuckled and held his hand. "You are my younger brother, Imran. I have never blamed you for anything. You should stop apologizing for others' deeds. I wish situations were different but…"

He nodded, his hair falling on his forehead as he swooped me in a hug. I sighed and hugged him back, wishing we had a better familial relationship.

"I know I can't help you with the proposal, but I have a small gift for you," he said, pulling away and handing me a piece of paper. I frowned, taking it and reading over it.

"It's a ticket."

"Ah, so you can read."

I pinched his arm and, ignoring his yelp, I said, "Why are you giving me a ticket to Azmia?"

"Because I want you to go have fun? It's a small gift for graduating with a master's degree in veterinary science."

"Aw, come here!" I hugged him again, cherishing the ticket as if it was a prized possession. No one had thought about gifting me anything but him.

"Wait, but why would you give me a ticket to Azmia? Father has a bad relationship with that country," I pointed out.

He winked at me. "What he doesn't know won't hurt him. Besides, tomorrow is their princess's birthday, so everyone will be busy celebrating. You can do whatever you want and have fun. No one will know who you are."

Imran was right. No one will know me. That I am Nasrin Elbaz, Princess of Maahnoor. I can go out, tour the capital and even spend the night out.

I kissed his cheek. "Thank you, Imran. You are the best brother anyone could ever have."

"You are exaggerating," he mumbled, smiling and wiping his cheek when he walked out of my room.

I knew in my heart that he would have been a far better choice as a Sultan of Maahnoor than Sadiq.

Looking down at the ticket, a grin tugged at my lips. I would be someone else for two days and have a taste of whatever freedom I could have.

3

ZAIN

My head was throbbing as I stepped inside the club. The guards kept their distance, but they followed me, doubling the protection around the club and the enormous expanse of the three floors. We owned several of the clubs and hotels in Azmia, especially the most popular in our capital, which celebrities used to party and forget about themselves without the fear of paparazzi.

My pace was steady, annoyance from the meeting with the twin princesses filling my steps as I made my way to the second floor. Red, blue, yellow and green neon lights danced through the dark walls covered in thin velvet fabric. People laughed, danced and made out against the obsidian pillars, the bartenders fulfilling the orders, our guards making sure everything went smoothly with no incident. I eyed the dance stage. People donned various dress shirts and short dresses dancing with their hands above their head, swaying to the upbeat music played by the DJ.

I felt envious, wishing I could go down and mingle with the crowd. Get drunk and dance and have a headache from the hangover, not from the stress of ruling the country, making sure I was the best every day.

Women giggled as they brushed past me, eyeing me. Color slashed my cheeks as I cleared my throat and climbed the stairs to reach the VIP floor. The bodyguard let me pass, my eyes taking in the circular tables, blood-colored couches, the exotic scent of the air.

"Well, well, well, look who showed up," Zayed whistled, his grin widening and dimples appearing in his cheeks. The blonde who was on his lap, kissing his neck moments ago, stood up when he whispered something in her ear. Her cheeks flushed when she walked past me, closing the door of the only private room on the VIP floor.

Only royals were allowed here. Me, Khalid, Zara, and our closest friend, the Sheikh of Azmia, Zayed.

"Where's Khalid?" I asked, sitting down and pouring myself a glass of whiskey.

Zayed kept grinning, and I rolled my eyes, swallowing the contents of the glass, the alcohol burning my throat. He was a year younger than me, similar to Khalid, so it was no wonder they were best mates. His dark curly hair fell over his forehead, charm exuding out of every pore of his tanned skin, his easygoing smile making both men and women envy him.

"He knew you'd come here," he said, clinking the bottle of champagne with my empty glass and drinking straight from it.

"So you knew about the princesses?"

"Of course, it was my plan after all." He gave me his shit-eating grin again and raised his brow. "So? What happened? Did you get laid, Your Highness?"

I gave him a deadpanned look.

Zayed pouted. "And here I thought you would like those

princesses. Would you prefer a prince instead? I know a few." His eyes twinkled at his own suggestion.

I looked away. Leave Zayed to know which princesses and princes were better in bed. "I am not into any of them. You know I am heterosexual. Quit being an ass."

"And asexual by the way you reacted towards those twins."

"How do you know that?" I asked, frowning.

He shrugged, "They told me. They were here moments ago with Khalid—"

"I don't want to hear about it," I interrupted him. "And there's nothing wrong with me being asexual. If I was asexual, that is."

Before Zayed could reply, the door of the private room opened, and I saw my brother, red smeared over his neck and the collar of his shirt as he tried to fix his hair.

"You are a dickhead," I said, greeting him.

Khalid straightened up hearing my voice and gave me a lazy shrug while he buttoned his shirt. Not realizing that the first two buttons were missing.

"I thought I was helping you out. Won't happen again, big brother."

"Sending two princesses to seduce me to have sex with them and marry them is not helping me out."

Zayed looked between us when I stood up, "Okay, calm down, you two."

I glared at my brother. "Stop interfering in my life, Khalid. I told you I don't want to marry."

He flared his nose at me. "And what is so wrong with that?"

I scoffed. "If you are so excited about marriage, then why don't you get married?"

"You guys are fighting for no reason, for fuck's sake," Zayed mumbled, drinking champagne.

"Shut up, Zayed." We both snapped in unison, glaring at him.

"I don't need heirs, Zain, you do," Khalid pointed at me. "Just marry someone and adopt a kid if you want to stay celibate. Don't force it on me."

"No one's forcing you to do anything, Khalid!" I yelled. "No one has told you to do anything for Azmia since I became a sultan. I never once asked for your help."

"Maybe it would be better if you did," Khalid said, his eyes dilated.

I swallowed the lump in my throat. "You know why I can't."

♛

"She is my daughter," our father said. "I will decide her future for the betterment of Azmia. She needs to accept the betrothal for our future."

"No, she does not." I glared at him, taking a step closer and trying to talk to him. Zara's cheeks were wet with tears. My heart thundering in my chest. "Let her go, *baba*. She is a kid."

He bellowed out, his face scrunched in anguish. "She is a monster! A witch! Ever since she was born, she has brought nothing but misery to our country. Our neighbors." His eyes turned red when he glared at her. "She killed my wives."

Zara shook her head, my heart breaking at the sight. She shouldn't hear such things from our father. He was angry and sad, trying to blame her for everything that had happened.

"I didn't k-kill them," she hiccupped, trying to get away from our father.

"Yes, you did! Maybe I should kill you too," he said, his lips curling in anger.

Khalid whispered beside me, "Please do something, Zain. He is… he is hurting her."

My eyes widened. I didn't want to believe it. All the rumors and concerned talk about my father going insane. But I was seeing it with my own eyes. Even though we bore the mark of his anger, I thought of him as the most powerful sultan, but seeing him trying to hurt my sister, his own daughter, for something we couldn't prevent from happening made it all clear.

"*Baba!* Stop!" I shouted, stepping between his hand that was going to strike my sister. I held in my wince when his palm hit my cheek, the pain ringing through my skin to my body as I took a step back, my arms protecting my sister.

"Stupid boy, move away!" He snapped, ready to strike again, and for the first time, I raised my arm to block his hit. I knew I would get punished for it later, but I wouldn't allow myself to watch him hurt another human being again. I couldn't allow that anymore. Not with Zara.

I gave him a little push, his hand wrapping around the cane he needed to use because of his old age and weak legs. The same cane that had been… no, I didn't have enough time to relive the past. I needed to make sure my brother and sister were safe. I broke the hold of his hand on her wrist and bristled at the red hand prints that marked the pale skin of my sister's arm.

It must have hurt her.

Swallowing my anger and hate, I crouched and wiped her tears. "Go with your brother Khalid. He will take you to your room, okay?"

She nodded, rushing towards Khalid, hugging his legs when he frowned at me and our father. "What are you doing, Zain?" he asked.

"I am making sure our father doesn't hurt anyone again," I said, glaring at the man who shared my blood.

Salman Al Latif laughed. There was something cruel and wicked about it. "You will hurt your father? Your own blood, boy? You can't even wield a sword properly and you dare talk back to me!"

I ignored my fear of backing away when he straightened his stance, his grey hair wild, his eyes even wilder when he looked at Zara, her little frame cowering behind Khalid's legs. Even he held his ground in front of our father.

"Come to your father, Zara," he yelled, rage filling his voice.

He didn't seem human anymore. He was the monster, driving away our mothers and hurting us.

"Khalid, take her away from here," I said, stopping him in his path.

He glared at me, raising his hand, which I held back with my strength. At least the lessons we had learned to fight wouldn't go to waste. I heard Khalid calling out my name, but it was too late.

I hissed in pain, dropping to my knees when his cane struck the back of my knee, my legs giving out underneath me. I held his leg when he tried to walk past me. "Don't be reckless, Father. She is your daughter."

He huffed, pulling his leg from my grip. "That monster is not my daughter. You should watch how you talk to me, boy; you don't want to end up like her, do you?"

I warned Khalid once again, not seeing the cane until it was too late. I squeezed my eyes shut when my head throbbed with the pain, my hand lifting to my head as I felt warm liquid rushing out. I blinked at the red coating my fingers, my vision blurring when I tried to stop him. Stop the monster my father had become.

But I couldn't.

When I managed to stand up, it was too late. Blood turned the Egyptian rug red, the guilty and scared look of

Khalid where he stood frozen in front of Zara's little body. Across him was the slumped body of our father, blood staining his tunic as Khalid pulled out the sword with weak hands. His voice was shaky when he whispered *'baba.'*

No, no, no.

I blinked again, staggering towards them and watching our father fall back on the rug, Khalid's eyes wide with shock as Zara tried her best to swallow her scream.

She hugged Khalid, my eyes averting to the sword dripping with crimson blood. I took it from his cold hand and whispered, "It's okay, Khalid. Zara. It's *okay.*"

Tears slid down my younger brother's face as he shook his head. "It's not. It's my fault. I… I killed—"

"No. *I* did." I forced out those words, holding the freezing sword in my hand.

I wouldn't let Khalid live with the blood of our father hanging over his head all his life. I would take the blame. I would get executed, knowing my brother and sister were safe.

His eyes widened, knowing what I was doing. Zara held my palm, her big hazel eyes gleaming with tears as she stared between the two of us. At least she wasn't hurt.

"It's okay, Khalid. Take care of Zara," I whispered, hearing the rush of footsteps coming towards the room.

Rahim opened the doors and before I could say anything, I heard a whisper and a shuffle, the sword being taken from me.

Khalid stood before me, my eyes wide with fear and shock when he said, "I did this. I killed my father. The Sultan of Azmia is dead."

KHALID LOOKED AT ME, HIS HEAD SHAKING. "YOU KNOW YOU don't have to do all of it by yourself, Zain."

"You have done enough, Khalid, I don't want to—"

"Do you blame yourself for what happened?" he asked.

Zayed took a sharp breath, standing up and knowing what we were talking about. He knew what had happened. He had followed Rahim that night and had seen everything.

I bit out, "You don't know what or how I feel when it comes to marrying and having children of my own."

"You are deflecting the subject, dear brother." Khalid took a step towards me, "You are not your—"

"You don't know what it feels like to be the Sultan, Khalid," I said, stopping whatever he wanted to say, pushing his shoulder as I walked past him and out of the room.

I didn't want to end up like my father. I didn't want to hurt my wife, my children and turn out to be like him. Or something worse.

The heady sound of the music made me feel present as I made my way downstairs. I needed something strong to drink. I needed to forget about that night. The scared expressions of Khalid and Zara. The guilt of not protecting them when they needed me the most. I needed to forget everything. Especially the pressing weight of getting married and siring children for the crown.

I weaved my way through the crowd to reach the bar. The club was more crowded than ever, everyone celebrating Zara's nineteenth birthday. Speaking of my sister, where was she? She had told us she would be in the club. Maybe I should check up on her first—

"You look so sexy," I heard a man slur, hiccupping when he tried to wrap his arm around a beautiful brunette dressed in a gorgeous black dress. Her golden skin glowed under the club lights.

"I am not interested," she said clearly, her voice sultry. Honeyed.

My palms started sweating. I frowned, looking at them. I hadn't even seen her face, and I was getting nervous. Shaking my head, I continued on my way, trying to ignore her when I heard the drunk man's words that made me stop dead in my tracks.

"Then why are you dressed like that?"

I spoke while walking towards them, "Because it's her body and she can dress however she wants." I glared at him, my voice loud and clear, "Leave before I call security and have you arrested."

He took a step back. "Who are you to step between us? I was just asking to dance with her."

My body hummed with satisfaction of fear that I was about to get when I parted my lips to answer his question. "I am the—"

But I never could finish my sentence.

"He is my husband, right, darling?"

4

NASRIN

I looked at the lavish interior of my hotel suite. Being a Princess of Maahnoor, I could afford to stay in a suite. The chilly breeze from the balcony ruffling my hair, laughter and music echoing in the city below. I averted my eyes to the suitcase beside the vanity. It was open, barely unpacked after arriving in Azmia for a night, using the ticket Imran had gifted me.

I ran a hand down my face, tucking the strands of my hair behind my ears. I needed to calm down and think. Be smart about the whole ridiculous ordeal. There must be a loophole.

You have to marry him. My father had said over the phone, his voice raspy with age, when I had landed in Azmia. I could hear the cruel smile in his voice. How I could ever be related to that man was a wonder on its own.

I couldn't escape to London anymore. I had a student loan to pay off and my father took care of the money that he allowed me to spend. I still had some little cash that I had earned during my part-time job at a vet clinic in London, but it wasn't enough to run away. Barely enough to survive.

Clenching my fists, I stood up from the bed and made my

way to the vanity mirror. Staring back at the angry dark eyes, I promised myself that I would never marry that old man or any other consorts of my father's choice. I won't let myself suffer again. I will fight him.

The emerald jewelry of my mother glinted with the light. The golden intricate design feeling soft against the pad of my finger and the huge emerald diamond, shaped as a dewdrop hanging below it. My mother's *maang tikka*. She had worn it as a family tradition during her wedding and gave it to me on her deathbed, promising me to wear it when I marry the person I love. She had regretted marrying my father, but she loved her children, loved us. So she wanted me not to repeat her mistake. Choose my heart over anything else.

I will keep that promise, Mother. Saying that to myself, I safely kept the jewelry in the drawer.

With a little hope, I stripped out of the jeans and tee shirt, donning a stunning black dress that felt liquid on my skin. Barely leaving anything to the imagination and accentuating my hips and curves, ending at my thigh. I adjusted the cleavage and the thin straps before applying minimal makeup.

Azmia was well known for its popular bars and clubs. Rumor had it that many celebrities and even royals themselves liked to party in the clubs. I could take a night off that I very well deserved and enjoy New Year's Eve.

♛

Tipping my head back, I swallowed the gin, licking my lips as I kept the glass on the counter. Pop music played in the background, people dancing and laughing on the stage, neon lights flashing over everyone's bodies, glistening with sweat. I eyed the throng of the strangers' faces, everyone enjoying in their own bubble, drinking, dancing, grinning.

Only half an hour left before the new year.

I hesitated only for a moment when the music changed to something heady, flowing between everyone, caressing my bare arms as if urging me to dance like a sensual lover. No one was going to give me another look here. No one knew that I was Princess Nasrin, the only Princess of Maahnoor. No one would care.

And if they did, they could very well go fuck themselves with a stick up their ass.

With my chin high, I stepped onto the dance floor, the music thrumming in my veins, the aftertaste of gin coating my mouth, encouraging me to close my eyes and move. Move my body the way I wanted it to, without the judgement of others. Just me and the music.

I danced, moving my hips and arms, caressing them with each new dance step, sweat coating my golden skin as I giggled and danced with three women. Our eyes bright as we swayed to the beat of the earthy, exotic music, getting lost in it.

"You look so sexy," a man slurred, hiccupping when he tried to wrap his arms around my waist.

Stepping back, I tried to ignore him, but he wouldn't budge. "I am not interested," I said clearly, batting away his hands that tried to touch me.

"Then why are you dressed like that?"

Oh, for the love of—

"Because it's her body and she can dress however she wants." I turned my head to the smoky voice of the most handsome man I had ever seen. He glared at the man and spoke with authority, "Leave before I call security and have you arrested."

I raised my brow when it seemed to work. The stranger took a step back, glancing between the two of us. "Who are you to step between us? I was just asking to dance with her."

The handsome stranger's eyes glittered, "I am the—"

"He is my husband, right, darling?" I smiled, leaning close to him.

"I am?" he questioned, tilting his head at me. The man scoffed, which made him glare at him again. "Yes, this beautiful woman is my wife. If you won't leave us, I will call security."

He left, leaving me with the handsome stranger.

He faced me, and my heart stuttered for a moment. His obsidian eyes pinned me in place while I tried not to trip in my heels, his tall, lean frame towering over me. The shirt he wore stretched over his broad shoulders, the shadows and lights of the club shadowing his chiseled sharp face. For a moment, I thought there was something familiar about him. My mind nagging at me to step back at the predatory glint in his eyes. Step back and hide myself.

But I didn't move.

I *couldn't* move.

I was in awe of his beauty. Captivated. The sheer power pouring out of him, people holding their breath when they looked between us. The music blurred out, as if I was underwater, shamelessly staring at the man who stood across from me. A head taller than me, even though I was tall for a female with the heels donning my feet. But he didn't make me feel small. No, he made me feel different. The feeling I couldn't put a finger on when he tipped my jaw towards him, the soft touch of his finger burning my skin, flaming it.

"You are *Limerence*," he spoke, his voice so deep and smooth that I wanted to sigh.

We were so close that my chest brushed his shirt. I took a deep breath, controlling myself from inviting him to my hotel room. By the way he expelled sheer male sexuality, everyone gawking at him with heart eyes. I knew he would be good—no, *terrific*, in bed.

I heard myself say, "What?"

He blinked at me, his long lashes making shadows on his sharp cheekbones. The dark slashing of his brows made his eyes seem hooded.

"Limerence, my wife," he replied in his husky voice.

My wife. My thighs clenched at the way he said it, so tenderly. His accent was laced with thick British English, as if he wasn't from here. But the tanned golden skin, his tousled dark hair and eyes pointed otherwise.

"Ten, nine, eight—"

We both broke out of the bubble at the same time, looking around to see people screaming down the numbers. *Right. It was New Year's Eve.*

"I want to kiss you," he said, looking me straight in the eye.

He didn't beat around the bush, did he?

"Five, four, three—"

"Please do," I whispered, wanting to kiss his full lips. I wanted to see how handsome his face would look from between my thighs or when I pleasure him, taking him in my mouth.

He hesitated, only for a second, before closing the distance between us and pressing his lips against mine. I lost all sense of being when everything but us melted into the shadows, cocooning ourselves in our bubble once again from the cheers and hoots of laughter. The kiss was soft, despite the passion and intensity promised in his eyes. I took the lead, closing my fingers around the lapel of his suit and pulling him closer, pressing our bodies against each other, his hard muscles against my soft curves. I deepened the kiss, nipping at his bottom lip and—

Oh.

A moan slipped past me when he wound his hand in my hair, his other hand lowering on my back and cupping my ass, giving it a light squeeze. He growled, the kiss getting hungrier with each second when we both tasted alcohol on each other's tongue.

I pulled away, my half-lidded eyes catching the sight of his flushed face. I knew I wanted to see that face, the face of my handsome husband, hovering above me.

Holding his hand, I whispered, "Come with me."

♔

It only took a couple of minutes to rush from the club towards the hotel. The heat from his muscular, lean body pressed against my back, his lips nibbling my ear when I tried to open the door to my suite. His soft chuckle rolling over my body, my thighs tensing at his husky voice when his hand snaked down to mine and slowly swiped the card, opening the door.

I pulled him inside with me, a gasp escaping my lips when he turned me around and pressed my back against the closed door. The handsome stranger swallowed my gasp, kissing me once more, his sensual lips moving to my jaw, down my neck while his hands roamed over my body.

His touch burning my skin. His lips searing me. His smoky scent turning me into mush.

Closing my eyes, I relished in the passion and possibilities of his hold. His strong hands touching me with the clear authority that he knew how that night would end. Naked in bed.

Before I could lead him to the bedroom, he pulled away. His warm breath caressing my cheeks. I loved how tender his hold was. Gentle yet firm.

"We should talk before we... we—"

"Yeah." I nodded, swallowing the lump in my throat. "Yes.

We should. You are my husband, I am your wife and we are celebrating the new year."

Despite the darkness of the hotel suite, I could feel him smile. Feel the intensity and pure lust gleaming in his eyes when he pressed closer, the hard muscles of his body against my soft curves.

I held back my whimper when he said, his voice rough, "Yeah? How are we going to celebrate it, wife?"

Licking my lips, I trailed my hands from his thick, soft hair down to the chiseled panes of his chest. He took in a sharp breath when I removed the suit jacket he was wearing, gliding my hands over the broad shoulders and to the collar of his shirt, slowly unbuttoning the buttons.

"I could show you how," I whispered, kissing his neck, pressing my lips down to his Adam's apple, licking it before I lowered my kisses.

"What's your name?" he asked, his breathing heavy when my knuckles brushed against the solid bulge of his arousal.

He is definitely well-endowed. Lucky me.

"Jasmine."

"Liar," he crooned in my ear, my toes curling in my heels when he dragged me from the hallway to the bedroom as if he knew the suite. "I meant your real name."

I watched his muscles move through the thin shirt when he closed the door behind us, my eyes landing on his sharp face, his eyes mischievous and inviting.

"If it's a one-night thing, then I don't see why you should know my real name," I said, removing the heels, trying hard not to shiver under his fiery gaze.

He didn't reply for a moment, and when I looked up, I could see his throat work, his lips glistening when he licked them. No one should look that good in dim light when they are doing nothing but thinking.

"My name is Zain," he introduced himself.

I raised my brow. "That's the name of the Sultan and it's his sister's birthday today."

"No way," he said, a small smile tugging at the corner of his lips when he removed his shirt. My eyes landed on the abs and the happy trail down his pants when he stepped closer. "What a coincidence."

I hummed, half-hearing what he said. I was too busy ogling his body, the sheer masculinity that oozed out of him. The air in the room hummed with sexual anticipation and all thoughts erased from my head when his lips claimed mine. My hands explored his body, touching the muscles and lowering to scratch his stomach. He groaned, the sound low and smoky, making heat curl between my legs.

A soft moan slipped past my lips when he squeezed my ass, pulling me so close that I could feel the hardness of his stiffened member against my thigh. My palm sought him out on its own. I wanted to feel him, touch him.

His eyes were dark and hooded with lust when I slowly squeezed his length, pulling him out of his boxers. I swallowed the lump in my throat at the naked sight of his dick. A bit of precum leaked from the tip when it stayed erect against his stomach.

I was snapped out of my ogling when Zain's hands fumbled with the straps of my dress. He helped me remove it, peeling the dress off my body, kissing the soft skin above my thong. I shivered when his fingers tweaked and rolled my hardened nipples, kissing them, biting them and leaving marks.

"Sit down," I whispered, pushing him on the edge of the bed. "I want to taste you."

Zain's cheeks flushed. It was both adorable and hot to see such a handsome man blush, watching me kneel between his powerful legs as if it was his first time. He had removed his pants and boxers, his dark eyes gazing at me, my sensitized breasts feeling heavy when he looked at them with bashful desire.

Licking my lips, I leaned closer and stroked his length, his velvety soft skin hardened in my palm. The soft sighs he made were a fuel to my arousal. My thong dampened with my juices, hearing the hot sounds he made when I licked him. The salty yet tangy taste of him erupting in my mouth as I hollowed out my cheeks and sucked.

"Oh, *fuck*," he groaned, his hand wrapping around my hair as I dipped down on his girthy length.

I hummed and moaned with him inside my mouth, my fingers tightening around his thighs as his hand curled around my head. I watched his exposed neck, the golden skin sporting a hickey. Pulling back, I took a deep breath.

"I will cum inside your mouth, wife," he whispered, his voice lowering an octave as he caressed my cheek, his own flushed red.

Shifting on my knees, I said, "I don't mind, husband."

Blood rushed to his face hearing me call him husband. Zain licked his lips. "Allow me to return the favor first."

But I want to make you come first.

Before I could voice it out, Zain picked me up and laid me down on the bed, as if I weighed nothing. The soft sheets were cool underneath my back, the sight of Zain hovering between my knees unnerving me.

My eyes widened when he slowly ran his finger from my slicked lips to the tiny bundle of nerves. A shiver of aching hunger rolled over my body, my thighs tensing and relaxing when he repeated his actions. I whimpered, raising my hips when he added another finger, toying around with my dripping need, spreading it around and watching every inch of my body react underneath his ministrations.

"Zain," I moaned when the soft pads of his fingers bumped against my clit, rolling it around, teasing me further.

His eyes flickered to me, gleaming with lust as he watched me and my fingers rolling around my hardened nipples. Licking his lips, he leaned down between the apex of my thighs. I took a shuddering breath, the air of the room heavy with pent-up sexual tension and pressing against my bare skin.

I bit my lip, muffling a gasp when Zain covered my burning sex with his fiery mouth. My back arched from the bed when his tongue licked and explored my most sensitive part. His hands held my thighs from snapping shut on his head, my hand threading into his thick hair when he kissed and laved at my pussy.

He hummed, my toes curling at the reverberations. I was moaning and sighing, my eyes pinned on his handsome face between my legs, my legs spreading wide over his broad shoulders, noticing the wicked delight of pleasure in his eyes when I groaned out his name.

Zain was wild. Nothing like the blushing, shy man I thought he was moments ago. He had turned into someone else, someone who took extreme pleasure while performing cunnillingus.

"I love your taste, wife," he whispered, letting my feet touch the mattress as he dipped his finger inside me, watching me bite my lip and push my hips towards him for more.

"More, Zain!" I pleaded with a broken moan, his lips wrapping around the bundle of nerves he was familiar with and sucking it in his mouth.

He inserted another finger inside me, my walls clenching around him, my body quivering when he curled his digits, touching the sensitive spot that made my mind turn blank.

I could feel his eyes on me when he repeated his actions, watching me grip the bedsheets, my groans pleading and broken from the need of release. I whined at the loss of his touch, my half-lidded eyes watching him lick his fingers before hovering above me.

We both took in a sharp breath when he rubbed the head of his glistening cock from my dripping slit to the bundle of nerves. I wrapped my arms around him, his lips planting on mine as we both swallowed each other's moans when he pushed himself inside me, my walls stretching against the little burn of his girthy length to accommodate him.

Zain cursed, his pupils dilated as he eyed both of us. Where we joined. I tried clenching him, his eyes widening as he elicited a groan, a hot red flush creeping up his neck to his face. I giggled, watching him with amusement. He was so raw and open with intimacy. I had never met anyone or at least slept with anyone who had shown those qualities.

It made me like him more—

No, Nasrin. You do not like a handsome stranger just because he is open, vocal and shows emotions while having sex.

I was quickly snapped out of my thoughts when he traced a finger from my cheek to my lips, gently caressing my face. It evoked a new aching feeling from deep within my heart that I didn't know whether to push him away or bury my face between his chest.

"Are you okay?" he asked, his voice barely audible.

I could feel him throbbing inside me. Surely, he must have wanted to fuck me and reach his climax. But he waited for my answer, assessing me with his intense eyes as if he was truly concerned about my well-being.

Don't make me like you.

I wanted to say, but I stuck with, "Yes, I am." Wrapping my legs around his muscular torso, I said, "Fuck me."

Zain's eyes darkened, his fingers clenching the bedsheet as he slowly retreated and slammed inside me, my lips parting into a soundless moan. *Holy shit.* Pleasure bloomed inside me at the feeling of fullness, my body trembling when Zain claimed me with each powerful thrust.

His hot groans and whispers were music to my ears. His jaw clenched when he gazed down at me, holding my hips to watch himself slide into me. It was extremely erotic to watch a man like him see himself sink into me, my nether lips soaking with arousal.

I moaned softly when his finger rubbed over my sensitive clit, his eyes drinking in all the little details. I groaned out, his dick plunging deep inside me, his heavy, powerful body pressing against me and claiming my lips with his.

"I am going to—" I uttered with a small groan, his fingers rubbing faster, his pace increasing as he swelled inside me.

Surprisingly, he came first, his climax erupting inside me as his face contorted into bliss, his fingers digging into my skin. I was in awe watching him, that my orgasm rocked my body. The scorching white hot lust swept through my body, my back arching and nails sinking into his back as I groaned out his name again and again. Holding onto him, gasping and writhing as my muscles contracted around him.

Zain gave one last thrust before collapsing beside me. We were out of breath, my ears ringing as I tried my best to regain control of my wild heartbeat. I was surprised when he pulled me closer, kissing my lips and running his hand through my hair and back. I was rendered speechless when Zain cuddled me. Laying his head on the crook of my neck, his fingers brushing the underside of my breast and the coarse hair of his legs pressed against mine.

If I hadn't been exhausted and deeply sated with the sex, I might have told him to leave or cover up. But I didn't. Because I didn't mind the warmth of his body, his soft breath fanning over my skin and the way he held me so close and tenderly that I would think that the night we had spent together meant more to him than me.

5

ZAIN

I hummed, burying my nose in the warm skin, taking a deep breath of the subtle scent of jasmine with something musky. Hair tickled my face, my hands gliding up the curve of soft skin. I squeezed the tenderness, opening my half-lidded eyes, and smiled.

Jasmine. That was the name of my wife. The beautiful brunette who was sleeping beside me. Her lips were parted as she breathed deeply, clutching the pillow and nuzzling her body towards mine.

A small smile made its way to my lips. It was three in the morning, white curtains flowing as the cool breeze swept into the room. Making sure not to wake her up, I shifted, pulling away from her, and stared up at the ceiling.

My thoughts were all over the place. I was conflicted, yet somehow relieved. I didn't know why. But the reality that I slept with her, a stranger, was like being splashed with a bucket of ice water on a winter night. Twenty-four hours ago, I didn't want to have sex. I was comfortable being abstinent all my life.

Yet, just one look at her. I couldn't stop myself.

Something shuffled. I looked down and mentally groaned, running a hand over my face. *I had to get hard at this hour.*

Surely it couldn't be because she's beautiful. There was something familiar about her, but I had been seduced by the most beautiful princesses and daughters of sheikhs and royals in the past since the day I was crowned as the Sultan. Then why did I lose all my senses as soon as I saw her?

Her face looked so serene when she was sleeping. The taste of her musky feminine scent lingered in my mouth, and I hated that I wanted to wake her up and taste her again. I hated that I was so physically attracted to her. A stranger. I hated that I wanted to have sex with her again and again and again until I had my fill. But the one thing that I hated the most was that I might never have my fill after what had happened a few hours ago.

Is this how my father felt when he saw my mother in the market? Saw her, wooed her, and married her? Only to harm her years later because he wasn't happy. Would I turn out just like him? Love someone and hurt them once I had enough?

How far does the apple fall from the tree?

"What are you thinking about?"

My eyes averted to the sultry voice of the woman staring up at me, her eyes half-lidded as she yawned, leaning closer. The subtle scent of jasmine wafted in my nose. I don't know why I wished to tell her the truth.

"I was thinking about my father. How… angry I am at him for being him, if that makes any sense," I said, my heart beat increasing waiting for her response. To laugh at my awkwardness and the fact that I was thinking about my father and my past when a stunning naked woman was sleeping beside me.

But she didn't laugh.

Her deep brown eyes blinked at me as she nodded. "Yes… I understand what you mean. I have a terrible relationship with my father." She grinned, poking my cheek with her finger, "In fact, you should be glad that I am angry at him."

"I should?"

"Yes. That's why I came to the club to drink and hopefully… you know." She looked around, waving her hand. My eyes dropping to her breasts when the blanket slid down.

I hummed, reaching my hand out to touch them. Her eyes flashing towards me, no longer sleepy as she bit her lip when my fingers rolled around the hardened nub.

"At least we have hateful fathers in common," I said, leaning down to kiss her neck, wrapping my hand around the back of her neck, and urging her closer. I hissed when she palmed my length. The blanket pushed away as we both sighed and moaned, teasing each other.

"Turn around," I whispered, my teeth grazing the shell of her ear.

Her eyes were wide with lust when she turned on her stomach, her arms and knees supporting her. My hands greedily trailed over her back, kissing the spine and fondling her breasts until she was bucking and moving back to have some friction. I spread her knees, settling myself between them.

"*Zain*," she said, her voice full of need when she pressed her ass back towards me.

She didn't need to plead again when I plunged myself inside her warm heat. The sounds of skin slapping against each other and our groans mingled together in the room. The air heavy with the musky scent of sex. I didn't stop moving inside her, holding her hips, her neck, her hair, kissing her until we both were sated and exhausted from the release.

I held her close, rubbing my hand on her back as we both slept peacefully in postcoital bliss.

♔

I DIDN'T PLAN TO WAKE UP BEFORE JASMINE. OR WHATEVER her name was. Watch the way her body was pressed against mine, her curves soft and inviting in the stream of morning sunlight that fell through the gaps of the curtains.

It was odd that I wanted to know things about her. Things like her favorite ice cream flavor. Which films she preferred. If she enjoyed horror or rom-com. If she was a night-owl or morning person. I wanted to wake her up and ask her.

Who are you? What do you do? Would like to go on a date—
Woah.

I sat up straight on the bed, my hand rubbing the little ache in my chest. Thankfully, she was still sleeping, her plum lips in a small pout as if she was angry at someone in her dreams.

Shaking my head, I got up, ignoring the loss of her warm body. I splashed my face with cold water and stared at my reflection. My hair was tousled, my eyes and face glowing. I traced the hickeys on my neck and collarbone with a small smirk. I had marked her body just like she had marked mine, and I wished I could wait and see how she would react to the indecent places I had left them.

But I knew I couldn't wait. I had an important physical training session with my trainer for the men's health column in a famous magazine and if I wasn't present, then it would be covered in the interview and media article. I couldn't tell them to reschedule it or Rahim would be disappointed in me.

As I got dressed, I thought back to Khalid's words last night. How I had taken a few more glasses of whiskey than necessary just to spite him. I felt childish, as if I was getting scolded by my father and not my brother.

Shaking off all those thoughts, I picked up her clothes from the floor and placed them on the armchair near the bed. Placing an order for a full breakfast for her, I gazed at her gorgeous face one last time, brushing a lock of dark hair behind her ear before leaving the bedroom.

Taking a piece of paper I wrote,

You were an amazing fuck. Let's not see each other again. Tootles xoxo with a little heart—

I am kidding. I am not a total asshole, I swear. Even though that is the exact sentence an asshole would say.

Instead, I wrote,

My lovely wife,

I apologize for leaving early without waking you up, darling. You looked simply too adorable, drooling on the pillow that I didn't want to wake you up. Yes, I took a picture and no, I won't delete it. Unless you wish to meet me again and ask me politely to delete it. Don't forget to finish your breakfast and I hope I get to see you soon.

Like a true romantic that I am, here's my email: zain.al@ azmiaemail.com

Your handsome husband,

Zain

Folding it neatly, I placed it on the coffee table and left her room before I regretted doing anything else.

6

NASRIN

Waking up to the empty bed was a bad feeling when I had the best sex of my life. That too, by a handsome stranger. But waking up to an empty bed and a dozen calls from your father and your brothers was worse.

"Did someone die?" I said as a greeting when Imran, my younger brother, picked up the call.

"Hello to you, too," he replied enthusiastically, which meant no one had died. How unfortunate. "No one has died. Yet. But you need to cut your visit short and come back home."

I resisted the urge to scoff at the palace he called home. The last time it had ever felt like home was the last night I spent with my mom on her deathbed. If I close my eyes and think hard enough, I can feel her hand gently stroking my hair, her soft voice before she closed her eyes and passed away early in the morning.

"Is it serious?" I asked, swallowing the lump in my throat and sitting up. The soreness between my legs was evident as

I tried to stifle my gasp, shuffling and sitting up in a comfortable position to relax the tensed muscles in my body.

"The Sheikh announced that you, well, more like Maahnoor, have to either accept or reject his proposal in two days." I could hear the guilt in his heavy voice. My hands clenching into a fist when he continued, "If we fail to answer him, his city will stop the export of vegetables and fruits to our country."

"What? That's bullshit. He can't do that. He is a sheikh of a city. Sadiq is the sultan of a country. Does that fool not know the difference between the two?"

"Nasrin," he said. "You don't understand the influence he has. He is old. Older than father, so people are ready to take his side over ours. We have barely done anything for our country since mother… you know. People haven't forgotten that."

I squeezed my eyes shut to block out the memories. I blurted, "I… I will be there as soon as I can."

I ended the call before we could exchange goodbyes. If I sat on the bed and kept waiting for a miracle to help me through this, nothing would happen. I knew because I had waited for my mom's cancer to go away, but it never did. I had to go to Maahnoor and see for myself if there was a way out of it.

I had to try.

♛

THERE WAS A SMALL SMILE ON MY FACE SINCE I LEFT THE hotel suite in Azmia and closed the door to my room in the palace of Maahnoor. Night had fallen, yet the smile remained.

My lovely wife. Adorable drooling face. Handsome husband.

Fool. I was a complete fool to keep grinning wildly and

clutching the handwritten note to my chest like a teenage girl. We had promised it was a one-night thing. Then why did he have to write the note? I wanted to know what he was thinking when he wrote it, that too with his email.

He was a tease. Leaving it up to me to reach out to him if I wanted to.

Of course, I wouldn't send him an email. That seemed utterly ridiculous. I had more serious matters to worry about, like the marriage proposal of a sheikh who could put a wedge between the city and the people of Maahnoor. I didn't have the time to think about the subject of the email or what to write or if I should tell him my identity, that I am a princess—

"No, you can't," I talked to myself, shaking my head at my reflection in the mirror.

There was already animosity between the two countries and I didn't know if he was from Azmia, Maahnoor or another country. I couldn't risk telling him my identity. That too, over an email.

I needed the night off to process and think of a plan to reject the marriage proposal and keep the unity of the people of Maahnoor at the same time.

Opening the drawer of my old vanity dresser, I opened the ruby box where I kept my mother's *maang tikka*. The only sentimental piece that belonged to my mother passed down to me. Promising me to marry the person I wanted to. Without thinking too much about the politics or religion or other's commands.

I pried open the lid, my eyes widening at the empty content of the box. Then I remembered sliding it in my bag before I left for Azmia. But I had kept it in the bedroom's dresser in a hotel suite, and I hadn't checked every drawer because I was in a hurry to pack up and leave.

I gaped at myself. I did not just lose my mother's most

precious sentimental piece of jewelry.

7

ZAIN

"Khalid, open the door before I break it!"

My guards had been waiting for me outside Jasmine's suite when I left, asking me if I was okay. Which I was. I had finished the physical training session and answered the questions about my diet to the interviewer even though I wished I was with *her*, feeding sliced mangoes to her.

Rahim had found me after the interview with the magazine, asking me if I had made the person whom I had slept with sign an NDA. After taking one look at my pale face, he asked me for a name which I swore I didn't know. His only question that bothered me the most was if I had used protection or not.

That was why I was panicking and forcing my brother to open the door to his room so I could ask for his help. I was sure he had forgotten all about our little chat back in the club the night before.

"Finally!" I said when the door opened, and my face dropped at the sight of the twin princesses. I blinked at them when they offered me a small wave and kissed my brother's cheek before walking out of his room.

"You look like you need something to drink," Khalid said, taking one look at me and tying his robe, allowing me to follow him inside.

"It's eleven in the morning," I deadpanned at the sunlight streaming inside his room. Fresh air breezed through the balcony that opened up to the gardens. My eyes ached at the sight of his messily organized room, the empty canvas by his bed is blank despite the colors he had poured out to paint.

He shrugged, filling a glass of water for me and whiskey for himself. "That has never stopped me."

Swallowing the water, I told him what had happened. How I had seen her in the club, kissed her, and spent the night with her. I ignored the gleeful look on his face when he found out I had sex and told him about me not thinking about the NDA, her real name, or that I had forgotten whether we had used protection. I didn't tell him about the email. That I had written my own email on a piece of paper that can allow anyone into the secure database used by the royals.

As a royal, it was necessary to get an NDA signed by the partner who will have a physical relationship with you. It was for the safety and privacy of ourselves and the country. If the person doesn't sign the NDA, we won't have any form of relationship from there on. Even the twin princesses must have signed them to spend the night in Khalid's bed, and vice versa.

"So, what do you think I..." I fumbled over my words, unable to bear to face him.

"I have the paintings of all the sex anatomy we used to educate Zara when she was eleven. Do you want me to explain what—"

"I know what happened, Khalid." I exclaimed, holding my head. "I know what sex is, for fuck's sake."

"I needed to make sure because you are blushing and talking about it like a shy virgin," he announced. "Oh, wait, you were a virgin until last night."

I didn't reply. My head was exploding. My heart was exploding. My stomach, thankfully, didn't feel like it was going to explode. All I could think about was protection. Not getting that woman, my fake-wife, Jasmine, pregnant. I didn't want to get anyone pregnant.

Ugh, why did I have sex? Because I was thinking with my other head.

"You seriously don't remember using a condom?" Khalid asked, concern lacing his voice.

I closed my eyes and shook my head. "I remember stopping this guy who wanted to touch her. She told him no, and he didn't seem to listen. When I stepped in, she introduced me as her husband—"

"Interesting."

"And she looked so sweet and beautiful that I called her my wife and… said something and we kissed. I remember that vividly." I didn't add that it was the best kiss I have ever had. If I touched my lips, I could still feel her there. Soft and pliant and enthralling.

That one kiss had ruined me.

"By the hickeys on your neck, I can assume things went past kissing?"

"Yes." I rubbed them, the warm tingle on my neck. It went way past kissing. "I am afraid that I didn't use any protection."

"*Fuck…*"

"Fuck indeed," I groaned and ran a hand through my hair.

"Do you know her name?"

"I don't know her name. We kept up with our husband-

and-wife roles. She told me her name was Jasmine but I am sure it's not her true name." I sheepishly added, "But I said my name was Zain."

My brother laughed, my shoulders slumping as I shook my head. Just one night of forgetting that I was a sultan and I am in a mess.

"And you didn't even remember about the NDA?"

I sighed, meeting his gaze.

Khalid gave me a look after swallowing the whiskey. "You are so bad at this, brother. If you don't remember using protection, then we have only one option."

"What?"

"We ask *her*."

⚜

IT HAD BEEN TWO DAYS SINCE MY SISTER'S NINETEENTH birthday. Zara had seemed a little distant, but Khalid and I thought it would be best to give her space until she came and talked to us about what bothered her.

We had gone back to the hotel room after lunch with guards flanking us. But we were too late. The woman in gold had vanished. There was no trace of her except the hint of jasmine in the air. The irony.

I had scoffed when I checked her name on the hotel guest list. She had checked in as Jasmine. I knew it was a false name, even though it suited her well. But she *wasn't* Jasmine.

I had found only one thing from that hotel room that assured me that that night wasn't any dream. That I had tasted heaven when I had kissed her.

A golden intricate piece of jewelry with an emerald placed as a dewdrop. It was a *maang tikka*. A traditional piece of head jewelry that would sell for more than the hotel building I had been standing in.

I had kept it to myself, making sure I didn't ruin it, and wondered about the name of its owner. The woman in gold. My pretend-wife for the night.

I could do a small interview in the media and ask the woman herself to step forward to claim it and privately talk to her about that night. But I couldn't do it, I didn't want to make that matter public. That I, Sultan of Azmia, didn't remember if I had used protection during sex or not. I didn't want any scandals attached to my name or hers.

The worst part about all of it was that I hadn't received any sort of anonymous email.

8

ZAIN

"What is that you are staring at, boy?"

I smiled at my *jadati* (grandmother) who slowly walked towards the dining room. I held her hand as she was seated in a chair, her dark brown eyes fixing on the beautiful piece of jewelry.

"Hmm," she grunted. "Are you asking someone for marriage?"

"No," I said. "I, uh, found this in a drawer of the hotel room. It seemed too precious to let the hotel staff handle it. We are trying to find the owner and return it."

I half lied, praying she wouldn't pick up on it and pinch my ears.

"I have seen a similar piece. This looks just like that with the emerald."

My heart rate picked up. "Where, *jadati*?"

She eyed the *maang tikka* and looked at me. "Sultana of Maahnoor used to wear it back when your father and Hamid Elbaz were friendly neighbors rather than enemies."

I clenched my jaw thinking about Maahnoor, our neighboring country. Once, a decade ago, it used to be famous for its beautiful sunsets, shimmering palace, sweet foods and jewelry with intricate designs like the one I held. But that was before Hamid Elbaz became corrupted, ruling it, taking the name of Maahnoor to shreds.

I shook off the animosity between Azmia and Maahnoor and asked my grandmother, "If Sultana wore it, then it must have been kept in the palace?"

I looked at the jewelry again. Was the woman in gold truly the owner of a royal heirloom?

"Rumor has it that she gave it to her daughter before she passed away," Grandma tsked, shaking her head. "Poor daughter was left alone in that palace with her three brothers and Hamid. I wonder what she is doing nowadays."

"You mean the Princess?"

"Who else, boy? That *maang tikka* belongs to Princess Nasrin Elbaz of Maahnoor," she said. "You better return it to her, ignoring the animosity between the two countries for this instant. It must be very dear to her."

Princess Nasrin…

My heart fell to my stomach as I stared in horror at the emerald diamond and the golden jewelry. It belonged to the Princess of Maahnoor, daughter of Hamid Elbaz. My father's nemesis, that meant my nemesis. My country's nemesis.

I certainly couldn't have picked a better partner to have sex with, even if I wanted.

♛

"ARE YOU SURE THEY DO NOT HAVE ANY WEAPONS WITH THEM?" Zayed, my brother's close friend and the Sheikh of Azmia, asked Rahim in a weary tone.

It had been a week since I'd learned that the *maang tikka* belonged to Princess Nasrin and I may have slept with her. Without protection.

I had invited Hamid Elbaz, her father, and the Princess herself to the palace for a meeting. A meeting was not the term my advisor, Rahim, would use. He made sure it seemed more like a talk for marriage between me and Nasrin. I had scoffed at that idea. I could never marry someone from Maahnoor, let alone their princess. The reason was my annoyance towards Hamid Elbaz and the current Sultan of Maahnoor, his eldest son, who was accused of sexual harassment towards a young man.

Also, there was that little hatred brimming between our two countries. I didn't know the details of what happened between my father and her father, but it was enough to make me aware that if I married Nasrin, people would talk. Wondering why I bothered to marry a princess from Maahnoor when I was getting marriage proposals from far better countries.

I couldn't marry her. As the Sultan of Azmia, I had to think of the future of my country.

That was also the reason I couldn't allow Princess Nasrin to turn that night into a scandal. Tell the public that Zain Al Latif was a clumsy drunk in bed and forgot to use protection. It would embarrass me and my entire family.

No, I couldn't let that happen. I wouldn't let that happen.

"Zayed, stand down," I said, straightening my suit. The golden embroidery on the lapels shimmered under the lights of the chandelier, in contrast against the dark onyx color of the suit. "It's just me and the Princess talking. Nothing else. Rahim said he would take care of her father or I will propose a walk in the gardens."

"Secure more guards in the garden—" Zayed ordered the guard present in my room as I scowled at my reflection.

"You're overthinking this," I said, sliding my family ring, a silver band around a dark cobalt diamond, on my right ring finger. I checked if the dagger was in place around my hip, sheathed and well hidden under the suit. It was for extra protection, even though I wished I wouldn't need to use it.

"They're here, Sultan," Rahim knocked on the open door of my room, tilting his head.

Taking a deep breath, I followed my advisor to the mahogany doors of a private library. The guards stationed outside opened the doors for us and I prowled inside. My stance relaxed even though my muscles were tight with tension.

My mouth turned dry when my eyes landed on the Princess. Her thick dark hair tumbled over her sun-kissed arms, her sharp face staring in my direction, her honeyed eyes pinned on me. They looked amused. Her red lips—the ones that I had kissed—curling at the corner. Despite that, I found Nasrin enchanting. A true beauty. Dressed in a shimmering golden gown.

The woman in gold was not a dream. She was real. I had kissed her.

Curse me. I wanted to kiss her again. Wipe that smug look off her face and pin her across the plush settee she sat on and kiss her. Mark her like some wild animal.

Just for a few moments, I wished our countries were not enemies so that I could propose marriage to her.

I am going insane.

Controlling my hormones, I smiled at her, ignoring her father, who sat on the armchair, frowning at me for not addressing him while Rahim gave our introductions.

"Sultan Zain, it's an honor to meet you," Hamid Elbaz lied, bowing his head when I stepped closer to the table covered in sweets for our guests. When Nasrin didn't avert her eyes from me to introduce herself, her father hissed her name.

I didn't miss the little note of disgust in his voice when he addressed her so brazenly in front of me. Interesting, a father who had a strong dislike towards his daughter. I could see why Salman Al Latif was a good friend with him before their rivalry.

Nasrin stood up, her dress swishing with each move when she bowed. "Honor to meet you, Sultan Zain," she said in her husky, smooth voice, as if she was caressing my cheek with her hand.

I stepped closer, the hint of fresh jasmine and a heady feminine scent wafting in my nose when I bowed, taking her palm in mine and gently brushing my lips over her knuckles.

"Pleasure is mine, Princess Nasrin," I whispered, rolling out her name on my tongue. Despite my deep-rooted values, I wanted to whisper her name, hear her gasping against mine when my fingers were deep inside her—

We both blinked when her father cleared his throat, displeasure written all over his face. I pulled away, the loss of her warm touch burning my palm as I slid my hand in my pocket. My fingers brushing over the cool jewelry.

There was so much tension hovering between us, that I was both afraid and excited to give us both some privacy. And ask her whether we used protection.

I asked her, "Would you like to take a walk with me in the gardens?"

"I don't think she should—"

I glared at Hamid Elbaz. "I asked Princess Nasrin. Not you."

He looked at me as if I thought of him like a piece of dirt on my shoe. "I was talking—"

"I can speak for myself, *baba*," Nasrin said, her eyes fleeting between her angered father and me. "I would love to walk with you, Sultan Zain. Please lead the way."

9

NASRIN

The soles of my golden flats and his shiny dark shoes made little to no sound when we walked together on the marble floors of the palace hallway. I couldn't keep from internally being in awe at every minute detail in the structure of the pillars, the domes, the antique decorations. Each and every little thing gleamed of opulence. Richness.

No wonder Azmia was well-known as the Golden country.

I had slept with the sultan of the country that bleeds gold, and he had an adorable picture of me drooling on his phone. I certainly knew how to pick a one-night stand.

Biting my cheek, I tried to look anywhere but at him. His presence and his aura were a living thing, beckoning me to gaze at him, marvel at his beauty and his leadership. I had seen no one talk like that to my father. Other than me, of course.

"The palace gardens are this way," Zain said, his voice husky, reminding me of the night we had spent together.

I followed him, shamelessly staring at the tailor-made suit

and pants he wore. The dark velvet suit looked marvelous on him. The golden embroidery with minute details donned the lapels of the suit, and the cuffs in intricate designs gleamed under the moonlight. I couldn't stop staring at how captivating he looked.

The night air was chilly, and the moon was bright, glowing, while two guards trailed behind us with lanterns, giving us enough privacy to talk. The garden seemed quiet in the night, bushes trimmed expertly in various shapes, the pathway paved with cobblestones.

I tried not to gawk at the tall, handsome man beside me, who smelled of musky pine and something heady. He was beautiful, radiating power and control with his lean, muscled frame. His wavy hair was pushed out of his face, the dark locks gleaming in the moonlight. Brows dark and slashing over his hooded obsidian pools of eyes.

I had tried my best not to tremble when he had seen me in the library with such intensity that I wanted to hide behind the curtains or run away from the palace. He had truly seen me. Just like the night we had kissed.

I wonder if he remembered that kiss and the night we spent together. The kiss that had ruined me.

"I wanted to talk to you about that night," Sultan Zain said. The timber of his smooth voice making me shiver.

I licked my lips, waiting for him to continue.

Zain stopped walking and turned towards me. I met his stare as he cleared his throat and asked, "Did we… did we use protection that night?"

I blinked. "What?" My mind went blank with confusion. "Are you asking me if we used protection—a condom or not?"

He didn't reply.

I almost laughed. Almost because he looked wounded.

"Sultan Zain, I am not sure if you remember, but you

didn't have any condoms with you, and I mentioned I was on birth control pills," I said. "If you want, we can get our tests done."

"No, of course not. I trust you. Thank you for clarifying. I didn't remember using protection that night and I had to ask you." He confessed, his broad shoulders rigid.

Of course, he called me to his palace to ask me about protection. Why would I ever think that it was something more than that? He didn't even know I was the princess when we slept together. I certainly didn't remember that the Sultan of Azmia was that handsome. Even though he had told me his name was Zain.

"I knew your name wasn't Jasmine," Zain said softly, as if he could read my mind.

I swallowed the lump in my throat and met his eyes. "It is my middle name."

He tested it out, my name rolling out smoothly from his lips. "Nasrin Jasmine Elbaz."

I hoped that my hair would hide my flush.

"What else do you remember from that night, if I may ask, Sultan Zain?" I said, continuing to walk beside him while his thoughtful face gazed at the close buds of the flowers. The sharp jawline with stubble reminded me how that scruff had grazed the delicate skin of my neck and inner-thighs, teasing me and calling me his *wife*.

"You don't need to be formal with me, Princess Nasrin. You can call me Zain."

"Zain it is." I loved how his name rolled off of my tongue. "But you may not address me by my name yet."

He chuckled, the sound of his laugh making me shiver. I rubbed my arms. "I won't address you by your name, Princess, if that is your wish—oh, I am sorry, are you cold?"

Before I could deny him, he had already removed his luxurious suit jacket and placed it around my shoulders. I tried not to sigh when he stepped back, his musky male scent surrounding me.

It smelled divine. If I could, I would steal it and take it to Maahnoor and sleep, snuggling it like a creep.

"And to answer your previous question," Zain said, his voice lowering into a smooth purr. "I remember kissing those full lips of yours. Licking them until you begged me to follow you to your room."

I swallowed the gulp in my throat when I met his eyes. Dark obsidian orbs pooled with desire when they gazed between my lips and eyes. "And?" I breathed. "Do you remember what happened when we reached my suite?"

His eyes darkened with a gleam, and I knew he remembered it. Knowing that guards were way behind us, I stepped closer to him, remembering how tall he was as I leaned on my toes and whispered,

"I took you in my mouth and pleased you until you stopped me," I crooned, smiling at the tremble in his body. "Do you remember, Sultan Zain?"

His eyes slid over my face as if he was assessing his enemy. He tilted his head to the side, a lock of hair brushing his brow when he said, "Maybe I need to see you repeat it, Nasrin. Refresh my memories a bit. Or the night wasn't that special that I forgot about it. About how beautiful you must have looked donning nothing and kneeling in front of me."

The audacity—

Reining in my anger, I smiled and checked my fingernails, "Hmm, I wonder why you left me covered in hickeys then."

"I remember." His eyes lowering from my neck to my chest, my stomach tightening as he raked his gaze over my body. As if he could see through my clothes, remember how he had left love bites all around my breasts, my stomach, my inner thighs.

"I wish I could see them," he whispered to himself, my breath catching in my throat upon hearing him.

Zain smirked, noting the blush on my cheeks. Straightening up, he pulled out something from his pocket. I gaped when I saw the golden emerald jewelry. "I believe this belongs to you," he said, handing me the *maang tikka* that I had been searching for frantically since last week.

"Thank you," I heard myself say as I checked over my family heirloom, sighing in relief when it was all in one piece with no dents or discoloration. "I had been worried because I couldn't find it. How did you…"

"I went back to the suite to meet you." his neck turned red when he continued. "I wanted to ask you if we had used protection, but you had left. Vanished. But I found that jewelry in the vanity drawer and kept it with me."

"You went to the hotel to see me? Ask me about protection?"

"I am the Sultan of Azmia, Princess Nasrin. I needed to make sure I didn't have any… unexpected heirs or scandals."

I gazed at him and back at the emerald headpiece. I could understand why he would have gone to such a great measure to invite me and my father to his palace.

Despite the animosity between our countries, he took care of the *maang tikka* instead of bargaining for it like my father or Sadiq would do. He took care of my mother's *maang tikka*.

Stepping closer, I wrapped my arms around his waist. He stiffened. I whispered, "Thank you, Zain."

His muscles relaxed when I hugged him for one more moment, his warm hands pressing against my back before I pulled away. Daring a glance at him, I saw his eyes glinting at me with the same intensity as when he had kissed me.

"I wanted to—"

"I have a que—"

We both spoke in unison.

I broke the silence first. "You were saying?"

"Do you have anywhere important to go tomorrow?" he asked, his voice smooth in the crispy night air. The way he said it made me want to pull his suit closer to me, tightening my fingers on the soft fabric. "Or perhaps next week?"

"I have an important meeting with a professor tomorrow," I said. It wasn't an important meeting, just an online call that I had to take and ask if she received the sweets that I had sent to her in London.

"I would like you to cancel it."

The close buds of the flowers whispered against each other when a chill night air flew through us. I tucked my hair behind my ear and peered at him. "Why would I do that, Zain?"

The glowing lantern cast a warm shadow on the sides of his face, making him look like some kind of king with the beautiful night as the backdrop. If I had the skill, I would have painted his portrait and called it the King of the Night. He truly looked like one, his dark eyes matching the sky.

Zain Al Latif stepped closer, his warm breath caressing my cheek as he said, "Because, Princess Nasrin, I am asking you to marry me."

10

ZAIN

"Because, Princess Nasrin, I am asking you to marry me," I said, my voice echoing in the dark night.

Her lush lips parted when she gaped at me. Even shocked, she was a stunning beauty. I hadn't been able to form any coherent words when I had seen her sitting in the library, her thick hair flowing down her waist, making me want to run my hand through it. Hold it as I whispered filthy things in her ear. What I would do to her if we were alone.

Her dark eyes glared at me through the surrounding kohl, illuminating her brown orbs. "Are you asking or ordering, Sultan?" She asked, her tone mocking when she tried so hard not to reject me.

I adored it.

The way she talked back to me, wanting to reject my proposal with defiance in her eyes. Maybe I was foolish, but I wanted to marry her, see the fire in her eyes every time I wake up next to her.

"I am asking, Princess Nasrin." I smiled at her, "For now."

Her chest heaved when she took a step closer to me, my

eyes dropping low at the exposed cleavage before landing on her beautiful, angry face. "Are you threatening me, Zain? Blackmailing the Princess of Maahnoor to get married?"

I blinked innocently at her. "I have done nothing of that sort, Princess, but I would if you do not accept my proposal."

"Truly romantic. I am swooning," Nasrin said with a smile dripping with venom.

"I wish I could have asked you in better circumstances, but time is of the essence."

"No, it's certainly not. And I am rejecting your sad excuse of a proposal," she snapped, ready to leave with my suit still draped around her shoulders.

I wanted to hold her arm, but I didn't want to get kicked in the crotch so I said, "It is either me or that sad excuse of a sheikh, Nasrin."

She stopped in her tracks, her golden gown shimmering in the moonlight.

Knowing I had her, I continued, "Remind me, Princess, how old is he again? Fifty-four, was it? No, no, I think it was sixty-four—"

"*Stop*," she hissed, the guards giving her an incredulous look when she marched in front of me. Anger rolled off of her in waves. "How do you know about that?"

"That you are not getting any suitors because of that pretty tongue of yours, Princess Nasrin?" I drawled.

Her eyes turned feral.

"I like to know about people with whom I share my bed, and the rumors of Princess Nasrin denying every proposal that comes her way are pretty famous. I know for a fact that you have denied princes and made them so angry after your rejection that only an old sheikh with two wives wants to marry you." I raked my eyes over her slim build, "And that too for your youth."

She seethed. "What's your point, Sultan? You don't want to cry in your bed after getting rejected by me?"

"Oh, you won't reject me, Nasrin," I said, leaning closer. "Because you *will* be my wife."

"T-that is not true, I…"

I tilted my head for her to continue when she flared her nose at me. She was furious, but she knew I was right. Having a little pity on her, I stepped back and asked,

"What is that you were going to ask me? Before I asked you for the marriage?"

"Does it matter now?"

"Yes, it does matter to me."

She gave me a wary look. "I was going to ask if you had found or chosen any bride yet."

So she knew I had been looking for a bride.

"I have." I looked straight at her with burning brown eyes. "Now."

"Why are you doing all of this, Zain?" she asked, her voice lowering that pulled at my stomach. "I am a lowly princess from Maahnoor. Surely women must be begging you on their knees to be your wife. Our countries are sworn enemies, and yet here you are."

"You are not a lowly princess, Nasrin. The history between Azmia and Maahnoor runs deeper than you know. If you accept my proposal, it will benefit our countries for the better." I took her palm, ignoring her warm touch, and lightly brushed my lips over her knuckles. "You have until tomorrow to think about this, or I will have to take measures and matters into my own hands, Princess."

I stepped back, turning my back on her when she asked, "What will those measures include?"

Staring straight at her, I said, "Dethroning your eldest brother from being the Sultan of Maahnoor and making sure no one but that sheikh has a marriage proposal for you." I removed an imaginary speck of lint from my black shirt and continued, "We both know your father enough that he'd accept the Sheikh's proposal. I am giving you a choice, Nasrin."

"It's not a choice if it's between that sheikh and you." she clenched her jaw, her eyes gleaming. "You are being cruel."

I stared at her. Maybe I was. How far does the apple fall from its tree? "Maybe. But I am not marrying for the same reason that sheikh is. I do not... want to force you into a physical marriage."

Nasrin frowned, her eyes gliding over my body. Crossing her arms, she raised her chin and asked, "Then? Why would you marry me?"

I cleared my throat, raking a hand through my hair. "You are beautiful, Nasrin. You must know that. But I don't care about your physical attributes. I have to get married, get a wife, a sultana. The animosity between our countries will end with you being the Sultana of Azmia."

Silence hung between us, the guards shuffling a few yards away. They couldn't hear us, but they must have felt the hovering tension between us.

"Will you," she took a deep breath and stepped closer, "Will you help me dethrone my eldest brother?"

Amusement glinted in my eyes as I raised my brow.

Nasrin continued, "We both know why you want to dethrone him. He has made terrible mistakes as the Sultan of Maahnoor and harassing a young man. That was the last straw. My younger brother, Imran, he will be a far better sultan, Zain."

I gazed at her dark eyes, fueled with determination to do the right thing. I leaned down and purred against her cheek, "If you become a sultana, *my wife*, you can do anything you want, Nasrin."

She took a shuddering breath when I pulled away. "I would need to think about it."

"You have until tomorrow."

Her eyes blazed, "Do not force me into this marriage, Zain."

I took a sharp breath and glared at her, her eyes blinking back at me as if it shocked her. Her words had cut right through me.

"I won't wait more than a week," I said, and walked away without giving her a second look. The guards stayed with her while I made my way to my room.

She didn't know how much her words had hurt. A stab to my heart.

Those were the same words I had heard my mother speak, sobbing through tears when me and Khalid would try to console her after our father's cruelty. She would weep silently, running her hands through our hair, having little Khalid sit on her lap because he was scared and tell us how he had forced her to get married.

My father had seen my mother in the market, called it love, and ordered her to accept his hand in marriage. She was wooed by his charms, but didn't know she was selling her body and soul to a devil until it was too late.

Do not force me into this marriage, Zain.

Nasrin's sharp words echoed in my head when sleep came to me at the darkest hour, hoping I wouldn't wake up with another twisted nightmare. Because I had become the only person I hated in the world.

My father.

11

NASRIN

"Arrogant prick," I grumbled under my breath when I rushed towards the palace, far away from the man who would be my husband in a few weeks if I accept his marriage proposal. Even his stupid, divine smelling suit reminded me of his handsome half-smirk. As if he knew I wouldn't reject him. Couldn't reject him.

But deep down, I knew he was right. All Zain was doing was being honest with me, and I hated how bitter the truth was. I knew that my beautiful country, Maahnoor, was not in good hands when my father appointed my eldest brother, Sadiq, as the sultan. He had made it unbearable for women to work, building clubs and bars when there was a need to build solid roads and schools for girls.

Not to mention about my rejection towards all the proposals that no one but a sixty-four-year-old man wanted me. Him or Sultan of Azmia. Despite being thirty-three, Zain had rejected all the proposals from the princesses to rich daughters of sheikhs, royals and even commoners. He didn't want to marry, so why would he propose to me after knowing me for barely a few days?

I would be stupid if I considered rejecting Zain's proposal of marriage. Being his wife, I could at least have a better future for my family and possibly my country.

But that meant I wouldn't keep the death promise of my mother. I won't be able to wear the *maang tikka*, which Zain took care of when I had lost it, if I accepted his marriage proposal. I didn't love him. I was attracted to him, I would be foolish not to accept *that*. He was a just, powerful ruler, far better than my father and brother, even outrunning the neighboring countries. He was a decent human being. He hadn't touched me without my consent when we both had been drunk that night. Not to mention his looks. Princesses were ready to kneel on his dais if he looked at them. Sharp face, dark brows, full lips and his onyx, haunting eyes were enough to curl up beside him, ask him about his day, relieve his stress of being a sultan and cuddle him.

Not like I had dreamt about it.

Or that kiss.

Or that nigh—

I stumbled into someone. Warm liquid drenched the front of their suit. *Oh shit.* That looked expensive.

"I am so sorry. I wasn't looking where I was going."

"Yes, you weren't looking, but no need to worry about— oh, *hello*."

I looked at the face of the man I had stumbled into.

"You are Khalid Al Latif. I adore *Limerence* and even have a small frame of it on my bedside!" I blurted like a fan girl, remembering how brilliant his paintings were.

"Thank you." He smiled at me as he tried to pat away the auburn liquid from his shirt with a cloth. I noticed the faint pink marks of lipstick on either side of his neck and shirt. "I am honored that you like my art, but if it's not too much, can

I ask who dared to make a beautiful princess angry in my castle?"

Ah, so he noticed me cursing.

"You can ask the Sultan."

He sighed, closing his eyes, and tried to offer me a sheepish smile. It was a wonder how similar both of them looked, but Khalid had more height and a muscular frame with gentle, kind eyes whereas Zain was tall with a lean muscular frame and cruel, obsidian eyes.

"If it helps, I deeply apologize on my brother's behalf. He doesn't know when to put a line between being a sultan and a decent human being," Khalid said, and called a guard to escort me to my room. "I will talk to him and punch some sense into him. Princess."

I bowed when he left, the guard leading me towards my room. How can two brothers be so different yet the same?

When the guard left, I shamelessly awed at the luxurious room. The king-size bed covered in golden satin with lace detailed fabric draping over the four-poster canopy bed. Even the pillow covers were etched with embroidery.

The closet was empty, with nothing but my bag of clothes. I removed my gown and sighed in relief, running my hand through my dark hair, brushing past my bare stomach. I wandered into the bath and discovered a whole new room of richness and earthy smelling oils.

After sinking myself into the warm bath, inhaling the sweet aroma of jasmine, I realized that this could be my life in a few weeks. *I can have all these luxuries and baths every day.*

The thought made me angry and sad. I wanted nothing to do with his riches. All I wanted to do was make Maahnoor a better country like it used to be and fulfill my mother's last wish.

I slept wearing a thin nightgown, the silk caressing my soft skin. I had decided. I would find a way to live with Zain

Al Latif. If he wanted to use me for my own title of princess, then I would do the same.

♛

"You have such lovely thick hair, Princess. You should keep it loose for today's event," the maid announced, showing me the dresses and gowns that Zain had bought for me.

The maid had knocked at the door before dawn and I had opened it wearing a robe, yawning and blinking with confusion when she entered my room, two guards dropping the dresses on my bed and leaving us alone.

"What event?" I asked, trailing my hand over the different fabrics of the dresses.

"Your family is officially meeting with the Sultan's and dining together to discuss your future matters," she said with a teasing glint in her eyes.

"My future matters?"

She giggled, "I have heard rumors from others that you and Sultan are to be engaged after some guards saw you kiss in the garden."

My face turned red upon hearing her words.

"I would never kiss—" I wanted to finish the sentence, but it was a lie. I had kissed him. *Repeatedly* on New Year's Eve.

"Ignore my words, Princess. Don't pay them any heed. Those are just silly rumors. Let me get your bath ready and help you with—"

"There's no need. I have been doing it for all my life," I said. "Although, I have a small favor to ask you."

"Anything for you, Princess."

12

ZAIN

I was floating into the darkness, my body weightless as it moved like a merman in the water. The fog thick and heavy, my vision blurry when I watched the two little figures. The third figure bigger than the two of them, crouching to talk to them.

"No, sweet, it doesn't hurt much," she whispered, her voice soft as she caressed little Zain's cheek and ruffled Khalid's hair.

I frowned, my eyes on her swollen cheek.

Childhood me knew what had happened. He had seen it. Tried to stop it and had received a lashing of his own afterwards. "But I saw Father sl—"

"I fell down from the stairs, Zain," her voice wasn't soft anymore. It didn't have any emotions. "Take your brother Khalid with you. Quickly before your father finds the both of you and scolds you two."

"But I don't want to leave you," Khalid whined, his hands wrapping around her neck. "I don't want Father to hurt you."

The dark room blurred away, changed into the light room. I knew it was Zara's nursery. Khalid was watching over her and painting a baby elephant, her favorite animal, on a canvas. Little Zain was scowling at them, jealous of their relationship as he skimmed through the pages of the book that Rahim had given him, saying they were necessary for someone who would be the next sultan.

I jerked back when our mothers rushed into the room, hugging us all and kissing our cheeks. They ignored our demands to tell them what happened while I begged them not to leave, no voice coming out of my mouth. They couldn't hear me as they said their goodbyes, promising me to take care of my family before leaving.

I tried to hold their hands, stopping them but it went right through them. The room was changing as I started falling down, only to land in the shadowy halls of the Court Room. There, on the throne, my father's figure was hunched over the arms, his sobs echoing in the empty room. I looked again. It wasn't empty.

Two coffins were open, the bodies of my mothers covered in white sheets.

Bile rose in my mouth as I backed away, glaring at the man who cried for them.

"You don't deserve to mourn over them!" I shouted, rage pouring out of me. "You killed them. Mentally and emotionally, before they died in that stupid plane crash. You could have stopped them from going to London, but you were too busy giving us one of your lessons. I hate you." I landed on my knees, tears gleaming in my eyes.

"I wish I had killed you."

I floated once again, my eyes adjusting to the horror of that night. The night that still haunted me and my siblings.

But it wasn't Khalid pushing a sword through my father's body.

It was me, my own hands wrapped around the hilt of the sword, my eyes widening as I pushed the sharp end through

Nasrin's chest. Her deep brown eyes were wide with shock, tears sliding down her pale cheeks.

"No, no, no, I didn't…" I shuddered, trying to pull back the sword, but I kept pushing, the golden gown covered in blood red. "Please, no!"

Her cold fingers touched my cheek, my body freezing at her touch. Her skin was no longer golden, it was ashen. It looked brittle. In a raspy voice, she whispered, "I told you not to force me into this marriage, Zain. Look what you have done."

I yelled for help, Zara and Khalid shaking their heads at me, looking disappointed as they turned around and walked out of the room. I cried, trying to hold onto Nasrin's body when she fell down on her knees, her hand dropping from my cheek.

"This is the curse of our family, boy," Salman Al Latif said as he sat in the armchair of his room, watching me breathe air into her mouth, pumping her heart. "You will be the reason for her death."

"No!" I bellowed. "I am nothing like you. I won't kill her. I won't ever—"

"I was the reason behind your mothers' death, child. Apple doesn't fall far from the tree, little Zain. You are just like me. A monster—"

A loud gasp broke me out of the spell. My eyes widening as I blinked rapidly and looked at my surroundings. I was in my room. There was no one sitting in the armchair by the window. I was alone.

Sitting up, I wiped the tears from my cheek and ran a hand through my hair. Another nightmare. Only it was worse because I killed Nasrin in it. Taking a shaky breath, I swallowed two glasses of water and wiped down sweat from my chest, removing my tee shirt.

I had to sleep on the other side of the bed because it was

covered in my sweat, counting numbers in my head and wishing that I would get a couple hours of sleep before dawn. Without any nightmares plaguing me.

♔

THE DARK SUIT HUGGED MY FRAME WITH THE LITTLE SILVER threads embroidered beautifully on the lapels and the cuffs. My eyes seemed full of hate when I stared at my reflection, recalling last night and the nightmare.

The way I had been with Nasrin, manipulating her and forcing her to accept the marriage. Just like my father. The way I had looked into her burning brown eyes and threatened her brother, her future. The way I had disappointed Khalid…

Bile rose in my stomach.

My eyes averted towards the sword hung over an empty wall. I glared at it. The sharp blade was sheathed carefully in the white and golden sheath. I had to remind myself that it wasn't dripping with blood anymore. It did not stain the beige wall with a splatter of blood. But it was tainted with the curse that my father had passed on to all of us.

After all these years, I had tried to be better than him. A better brother. A better sultan. A better husband. But I was failing miserably, and we hadn't even been engaged yet. My fingers dug into my palm. The screams of agony of my mother echoing in my head, her silent cries when my father wasn't around, hiding her pain and suffering from us until he allowed her to fly and her dying in a plane crash.

I was ashamed and scared that I was doing the same to Nasrin.

Apple doesn't fall far from the tree, little Zain. You are just like me. A monster—

"No, I am not." I gritted my teeth, ignoring the taunting words of my dead father.

"Don't tell me you are drunk, Brother," Khalid said, sauntering into my room and glancing at the blank wall where I looked. His stark face morphed into anger. It hurt him the most. After all, the sword was the living reminder of the burden he shouldered for killing our father in front of me and Zara.

Guilt crashed into me, wishing I had shouldered that burden, protected us, protected Zara from that monster. Wishing I had killed that man and not Khalid. I would do anything to erase that pain from his eyes.

"You should burn that rotten thing," he said, his voice devoid of any emotion. "It stinks of that… man's cruelty."

"It's a family heirloom and tradition, Khalid."

He scoffed, walking towards me. He was wearing a darker suit, identical to mine. His eyes had bags underneath them, but he still looked handsome as ever.

"Family tradition, huh? Are you going to treat Nasrin the same way as father did to mo—"

"Watch. Your. Words," I snarled, stepping closer to him. He may be taller than me, had more muscles, but the way I glared at him made him look away. Anger coursed through my blood when I said, "I have never raised my hand to anyone, especially Nasrin. Nor will I ever. You would see me without my arms if I ever do."

He hummed mockingly, "Father never hit women, Zain. Not even mother until our second mother gave birth to Zara. It started then, you know, all the screams and cries we would hear. Probably still hear in our nightmares. We couldn't do anything but watch and get hit when we tried to stop him."

Khalid took a step towards me, his hazel eyes swirling with pain, which we both shared. "Do not make me cut your arms, because I will if you—"

I chuckled darkly, "Threatening your older brother like you did to our father?"

"*Stop.*"

We both pulled away before we could start fighting and looked at our little sister, her wide hazel eyes looking at both of us. We straightened ourselves, ready with an excuse—

"There's so much anger in both of your eyes that sometimes I wonder to myself that you are the same brothers who used to teach me how to paint and how to wield a sword," she said, wounding our pride and ego in one blow. "I heard you are getting engaged to Princess Nasrin today. Give these to her when you go visit her."

Zara dropped the bouquet of jasmine on the mahogany table, her feet stomping.

"Zara, wait, I need to talk to you about last night—" Khalid went after her, giving me one last look before leaving me alone in my room with the flowers.

I took a deep breath. If I had tried to be a better brother and better sultan, then there's nothing stopping me from being a better husband. I did not want to disappoint my late mothers, my brother, my little sister, myself and... especially Nasrin. She deserved better after living with the men she grew up with for twenty-six years.

I would give her a better life than she had ever dreamt of. After all, I was the Sultan of Azmia.

My palms were sweaty when I knocked on the door to Nasrin's room, the guards stationed outside hiding their smile when they saw the white flowers in my hand. I cleared my throat and waited for the door to open.

"Princess told us to let you in if you visit her... or her maid," one of the guards spoke.

Did she now? I stepped inside, locking the door behind me. Her room was clean, the subtle scent of jasmine and pine lingered in the fresh morning air, a warm breeze travelling through the open doors of the balcony into the room.

I glanced around. But she wasn't here—

"In here, Sultan," her husky voice poured out of the washroom.

My muscles tightened underneath my clothes. I could leave the flowers on the vanity dresser and ask her to talk with me later. But the way she called out to me... I was curious to know what she wanted to discuss with me in the bathroom, of all places.

I made my way towards it, mustering up courage when I realized the door was unlocked and anyone could have stepped inside. Swallowing, I pushed open the door. The exotic scent of bath oils wafted around the room, my eyes pinning on the woman taking a bath, submerged in the water, wearing nothing but a gorgeous smile.

"Good morning, Princess," I said, removing my suit when it got too warm with the steam. I eyed the edge of the bath, made from an obsidian solid stone, carved into the shape of a bath, smoothed from the inside.

Nasrin smiled, her eyes dancing over my body. "Good morning, Zain."

Fuck. Me.

The way she rolled out my name like a smooth purr had me tightening in my pants, hoping she couldn't see how much it affected me.

"I will wait outside—"

"Please, sit," she whispered, her golden arms glistening with water. I eyed the small stool near the bath and raised my brow at her. She continued, "Help me scrub my back, please."

She did not just use the word please twice in five seconds.

I knew she was up-to something.

Still, I sat on the stool, shamelessly eyeing her sun-kissed skin, and rolled the sleeves of my black shirt over my elbow. I didn't miss the way her warm brown eyes gazed at my arms, my hands, my fingers, as if she was wishing—

I clenched my jaw when I noticed the hardened peaks of her dusky nipples through the water. She came closer, her hair pinned up, eyes gleaming.

"I received the message from the maid to meet you, but I didn't think you would call the Sultan to scrub your back," I said, my voice lowering an octave when I took the loofah, wetting it and dropping a dollop of scented oil over it.

Nasrin teased, showing me her back, "This would be the least of your worries if we get married, Zain."

I paused, my eyes on her. "I wanted to apologize for my behavior last night."

"Huh."

Leaning forward, I gently touched the loofah to her skin, noticing the shudder running over her back when I moved it across her shoulders. "I mean it, Nasrin. I shouldn't have forced you to choose between me or that sheikh. Even if it's too late for it, I am deeply sorry for the way I treated you."

I took a deep breath, rubbing the lather over her spine. "You do not have to accept this marriage, if that's your wish."

PART II

"Every inch of you is divine."

13

NASRIN

I held in the tremble of my body when I felt the smooth surface of the loofah lowering to my spine. I wanted to arch my back and close my eyes and let him lather me with his veiny hands all day if he wished.

I was snapped out of my dirty thoughts when Zain said, "You do not have to accept this marriage, if that's your wish."

"What?" I turned around to see him. "What do you mean?"

I had been so surprised by his words that I had forgotten that I was in the bath. His face flamed when his eyes dropped below my chin, at my bare breasts. My heart thudded wildly when his obsidian eyes darkened, my nipples tightening and turning into hard peaks under his scorching gaze.

With flushed cheeks, he looked away, his hand tightening over the loofah he held. He gritted out, "You do not have to accept me as your husband. Reject me if you wish. I… I will help you find a better prince and help your younger brother be the sultan."

I swallowed the lump in my throat, lowering myself into

the bath. The warm water was turning cold as I thought about what he said. His apology, his behavior, his words.

Peering up at him, I asked, "Will a prince help me turn Maahnoor into a better country?"

Zain faced me, his eyes not lowering from my face. "Depends on which city's prince you marry, Nasrin. But if they tried, maybe they can help you."

I hummed, giving it another thought and answered with my chin high, "Then I do not wish to marry anyone else but you, Zain."

"Why?" He breathed.

I closed my hand around his, rubbing my thumb over his knuckles, his wrist with a gentle touch. "Because even though you were cruel last night, you were honest. And as much as I hated you for speaking the truth, I needed to hear it. I admire that about you."

"Hated?" he asked, raising his brow. "Past tense?"

"Yes, Zain." I dipped my chin, only a little. "But I have some conditions before I marry you."

His burning gaze danced over my body, underneath the water. My stomach dipped, the familiar pang of arousal tightening between my legs. I held my breath when Zain leaned closer, his eyes raising from my thighs to my face.

The musky, masculine scent of his cologne fused with the jasmine bath oil, creating a heady air around us. I took a deep breath, clenching my fists when he placed the loofah over the crook of my neck, slowly lathering the sensitive skin.

"Go on," he whispered, his warm breath brushing my cheek. My eyes fluttered close, hearing his deep baritone voice. "I am listening."

"I want to work after we get married," I said, forcing my eyelids to open, gazing at the delicious exposed tanned skin of his neck. A little closer and I would be able to lick it.

Zain hummed, the reverberations rumbling down my

spine making me clench my legs. "That can be arranged." The small quirk on his lips assured me he had noticed what his closeness did to me. "But you have to be present with me during the festivities or important meetings regarding Azmia and Maahnoor."

I hadn't expected that. Maybe Zain was truly a ruler, as everyone had been talking about.

"Even though I am a woman?" I asked, remembering the rejection of my father whenever I tried to enter a political meeting. That it was not a woman's place.

The loofah stopped on my collarbone, his eyes narrowing on me. "Being a female changes nothing. Azmia has better protection and laws for both the genders because of our women's council. I would like it if you can join the women's council after the marriage. It would help me with a few of the decisions."

I was in awe. It seemed like the person I had met the night before was just being a sultan, but the man in front of me was Sultan and human and Zain, caring about his people, their needs and wants.

"Of course, I will help you." I licked my lips, "It will be my honor."

He smiled, my heart tightening at the sight of it. Illegal, it should be illegal for Zain Al Latif to smile at me without giving me a warning. "You can work as a vet, I do not mind."

His charcoal eyes drifted to my collarbone, continuing his work when the loofah pressed just above my breasts. "But I won't allow my wife to overwork and strain her little body."

Heat burned between us, my chest arching for his touch. "So bossy, Sultan Zain."

"May I?" He asked, his eyes lowering to my hardened nipples.

I nodded, sitting straighter in the bath. Not because he asked me too, but because I wanted to. Okay, that was a poor lie. I wanted him to see me. See how much he affected me, even though he was bathing me fully clothed.

"If it's okay, I do not want you to get married again, and tell me before you get any mistresses." I looked down at the soapy water, not wanting him to see me. "Don't lie to me, Zain."

"I promise to stay monogamous throughout our entire marriage, Nasrin," he said, his voice firm with authority. I held in my gasp when his warm fingers held my jaw to make me look at him, his touch soft. "I don't wish to warm anyone's but your bed—*our* bed. And I would never lie to you, Princess."

I nodded, his eyes taking in my reaction. I knew he wasn't the type of man to have an affair or mistresses, but I had to be sure. I wanted to know if there was anyone else he cared about… or loved. Surely, he must have slept with more women than I can count on my fingers. He was the Sultan of the most powerful country in the Middle East after all, I had to know.

"Why do I feel that there is something else you want to say?" he urged, head tilting to the side.

In the dim light of the bathroom, the dark strands of his hair seemed tinted with blue, his sharp jaw and cheekbones making him look otherworldly. It intimidated me how easily I could forget that he was a sultan and I was a princess of the country he had a rivalry with. If he wished, he could marry me in a day and keep me in a dungeon, keep me caged. If he wished, he didn't have to accept my wishes, my conditions.

But he didn't.

I had to say it. Licking my lips, I parted them, my eyes burning when his lowered to my wet lips. "I don't want you to touch me without my consent."

Ice drenched his features when he stilled, the swirling emotions fading from his eyes as they turned cold. His hand pulled away, and I had the strangest urge to get closer and feel the warmth of his hand on my skin again.

Zain chuckled, his laugh devoid of any humor making me shudder. He leaned closer and my eyes widened when his lips went past mine to press against my ear as he whispered, "I don't want to know why you think so lowly of me, but I assure you, future *wife*…" A slither of pleasure rolled over my spine hearing his rumbling velvety voice, his lips brushing over the shell of my ear, "That you would be the one begging me to touch you."

He was so right, he had no idea.

I would beg. For him. *Only* him.

My eyes were glazed when they roved over his powerful, lean body, the muscles on his biceps moving when he leaned back on the stool. I pressed my teeth on my bottom lip, the air around us thickening with the steam, exotic oil, his musky cologne.

I met his eyes. "Then I beg you to touch me, Zain." I swallowed the lump in my throat and added in a soft whisper, "Please."

His eyes widened a little with shock, and something darker coursed through them. My heart thudded loudly when I realized what it was. Pure lust. Desire. If I could move back in the bath, I would, because his gaze turned predatory, and I felt like his prey. Naked in the bath, while he was covered in clothes.

I watched when he unbuttoned the top two buttons of his dark shirt, revealing the tan skin underneath. My tongue seeped out to wet my lips. A hint of a smirk grazed his lush lips when he said,

"Spread your legs and show me your cunt, Princess."

Shock spread through my body. His words… so dirty and wild for a sultan. I swallowed the lump in my throat, wondering if I had made a mistake in poking some primal beast.

I watched him stand up and remove his shirt, his eyebrow raising at me. Taking a deep breath, I followed his command, spreading my legs and blushing when his eyes landed on the apex of my thighs. His bulge hardening as he removed his pants and boxers, standing naked in front of me.

I licked my lips when he entered the bath, sitting down across from me.

"May I?" he asked, gesturing to my legs.

I nodded eagerly. Perhaps too eagerly. "Yes, please."

His large hands glided over my legs, goose bumps skittering all over my body when he leaned closer, spreading my thighs as wide as he could. The cold marble pressing against my skin.

I stifled my moan when his fingers ran over my slit, slowly, as if he had all the time in the world to tease me. "Tell me, Nasrin, what do you enjoy the most? Getting your clit rubbed?" He rubbed the sensitive bundle of nerves with his fingers, watching me tremble. "Or your cunt fucked?" he whispered, his voice hot and heavy as his fingers slid inside me.

My back arched and eyes squeezed shut when my walls clenched around his fingers, a soft moan passing through my lips. When I couldn't reply, he repeated his actions, fucking me with his fingers, curling them towards my G-spot.

"I don't like to repeat myself, Nasrin. Tell me."

"Both," I gasped, my eyes widening at him. "Both. I like both."

Zain nodded, his body wet with water as he teased me. The pad of his thumb slowly rubbing circles over my clit, his fingers plunging inside me. Having him watch me grind myself on his hand felt dirty, raw, and intimate. His onyx eyes raking over my body as if he was thinking about touching and licking me everywhere.

Our eyes lowered to his hand, already glistening with my juices as his own hardened member stood erect. I tried to lean closer to him and please him, but he shook his head, his eyes blazing with lust and hunger.

I held his cheek and claimed his lips, a pleasant hum pouring out of him. He pulled me closer, kissing me deeply and intensely when my orgasm tethered on the edge.

"Every inch of you is divine," Zain said, his voice thick.

I blushed, my neck and cheeks heating.

"I wish I could devour you right now and show you how much, Nasrin." his guttural voice rolled over my body, his face leaned closer until his lips landed on my neck, tasting the skin, licking it.

I closed my eyes, arching myself in his touch when his teeth pressed against the sensitive spot. "I am touching you because you begged me to. Because I want to lick your perfect breasts and bite them when you come for me. You will, won't you, Princess?" he whispered, my stomach tightening into a ball at his hot words.

My head dipped in a nod, my breathy whimper making him smile when he lowered his other hand into the water behind me, supporting my lower back. My hand moved on its own accord, holding onto his muscular forearm, veins moving when my fingers tightened over his tanned skin.

Zain hummed, his mouth lowering to my collarbone at the same time as his fingers thrust deeper, making me sigh at the slight relief. But it was short-lived when his hot mouth attached to my breast, his fiery tongue licking the pebbled nipple before his teeth bit into it.

I groaned his name, my half-lidded eyes gazing over his thick dark hair. Pleasure bubbled inside me at the familiar tightness. His mouth repeated the same actions on my other breast, the hand on my back rubbing slow circles as my orgasm climbed higher and higher until it reached its peak.

"Before you cum," Zain said, pulling away from my chest. He licked his pillowy lips, glancing at his fingers inside me. "I have my own conditions."

I gaped at him, wanting to strangle him with my bare hands for—

He smirked, as if he could read my mind. "Now, now, don't be angry. I will help you climax, Princess."

14

ZAIN

I had to fight off my grin, even though I felt a little guilty for stopping Nasrin from reaching her high. But I needed her to approve of my conditions for the marriage.

"Out with it," she said, glaring at me.

With little thought, I brought my glistening fingers to my mouth and tasted her. Met her wide eyes, groaning at the honeyed taste of her. So sweet. So heavenly.

I pulled back and licked my lips, her exotic taste lingering in my mouth. "One, I do not want you to have any lovers after marriage. Two, we sleep in the same room. Three, we use protection."

Her eyes blinked at me as if she was pulled out of some daze. Her beautiful caramel eyes narrowed at me. "Is that all?"

I nodded and shamelessly raked my eyes over her bare body. Blood flowing south in my body at the sight of her wet curves, her round breasts pink with my kissing and biting.

"I wish I could add another condition to have you naked

when we are alone, but I do not want to get kicked in my crotch," I confessed.

Her cheeks flamed, her eyes lowering to the said crotch, which made her neck flame red. She was flushing at the sight of my hardened dick pressing against my stomach.

Nasrin muttered quickly, "I accept your three conditions."

"Not the last one?" I urged.

"No," she mused. "You are so..."

"Irresistible?"

"No."

"Enchanting?"

"*No*. You are dirty and wild."

I narrowed my eyes at her and flicked my wrist in the water so that it splashed across her. She gaped at me as I muttered, "That was not nice of you."

She didn't reply. She cupped her palm in the water and before I could pull back, it splashed over my face, drenching my hair, too.

Taking a deep breath, I rubbed off the water from my face, glaring at Nasrin who was smiling at me. "That was definitely not nice of you," I whispered, holding her hand. I ignored her squeal of laughter as she closed her eyes, expecting to be held underwater in the bath.

But the sweet fool didn't know I was smiling at her scrunched face. Her beauty awed me. Her golden skin, her sharp cheekbones, full lips that were shut closed, hiding the toothy grin.

Nasrin finally opened her eyes, her pupils widening. Without another thought, I closed my eyes and claimed her soft lips with mine. I pulled her closer, her breasts pressing against my muscular chest. I breathed when her lips burned into mine in a sweet caress.

It wasn't like the kiss we had at the club. It was different. More intimate. More open. More passionate.

Our mouths explored each other, my hands gliding over her naked body, touching the wet naked skin while her fingers threaded in my hair. My stiffened length pressed against her legs, and I remembered how much she must be aching. How wet her pussy had been when I had interrupted her.

"Let me," I breathed, pulling away. "Let me make you come."

Her eyes had turned dark as she nodded, allowing my hand to dip between her legs again. My fingers rubbed over the slick juices of her arousal around her heated sex, noticing every pant and gasp escaping her red lips, swollen with kisses.

I supported her back with a hand, her chest flush against mine, feeling her thudding heart and ragged breathing. She tried to balance herself in the bath, but she knew I had her. I wouldn't let her slip and injure herself. I wanted to pull her onto my lap, but I was afraid that if I had her on my lap, I wouldn't be fucking her with just my fingers.

"Do you want me to fuck you like this, Nasrin?" I asked, my breathing harsh. "Do you want me to fuck your tight pussy with my fingers, *hm?*"

She nodded, her eyes closing shut when her hips pressed against my hand, riding herself on my palm. "Please," she whispered.

I nodded, knowing what she needed. What I needed. I pushed another finger inside her, stretching her as she groaned out my name against my neck. Nasrin arched her back, her legs trembling when I repeated my action. Playing with her clit, pressing against it while fucking her with my fingers. Her tight, velvety walls clamped around me, shivers of pleasure rolling down her spine as I held her close.

"Zain," she moaned, her voice soft and breathy. Her eyes

squeezed shut, her hips moving to meet the small thrusts of my fingers, thumb rolling over her clit.

I bit down on her nipple, sucking it in my hot mouth, groaning when she whimpered. Her sounds made me want to sin. The honeyed taste of her arousal tingled in my mouth, wishing I could pleasure her with my tongue and not just my fingers.

"C-close," she gasped, her fingernails digging into my arms. "So close."

I pulled back to lick and soothe the pinkish hue on her nipple, repeating my action on her other breast and curling my fingers inside her. She groaned, her body trembling as the pads of my fingers found the rough, sensitive spot I had read about. I noted her reactions and slowly did it again, her answering guttural moan assuring me to keep on repeating my actions.

"That's it, Nasrin," I breathed. "Come on my fingers."

She closed her eyes. My own averting to the warmth of her dripping sex, her walls clenching my fingers, clamping them. Her swollen clit red with the overstimulation, her slicked lips welcoming my fingers inside her, stretching her until she cursed, making a whimpering sound.

I pushed her closer, ordering her, "Open your eyes, Nasrin. Look at me."

Her auburn orbs peeked at me from half-lidded eyes, gold and dark brown dotting the surrounding crease of dark pupils. Her lips parted in a silent moan, her body thrumming with pleasure, easing with it when her orgasm reached its peak, her body tumbling over its edge.

I held her, watching in lustful awe at the beautiful woman, her golden skin rising with goose bumps when she came. Climaxed on my fingers, coating them with her glistening juices as I watched them disappear inside her, soothing her. Rubbing her back, I smoothed a few strands that had escaped from her bun, tucking them behind her ear when her body went through the aftershocks, a flushing glow radiating from her olive skin.

"So fucking beautiful," I said, watching her body react to my touch.

I loved seeing her like that. Seeing a stunning woman like her come apart in my hands, making her reach her high, watching the heavy rise and fall of her breasts, flushed with her recent orgasm.

Nuzzling her neck, I breathed in the jasmine with the feminine, musky scent. "I think you have made me an addict, Princess," I whispered in her ear. "I can't seem to have my fill after watching you come apart in my hands."

"*Zain...*" she hummed my name, the flush creeping over her arched neck and cheeks.

"I want to make you cum again."

15

NASRIN

My core burned hearing him, my body heating underneath his gleaming obsidian eyes. I couldn't believe that man. Sultan Zain Al Latif, my soon-to-be-husband, wanted to make me come again. It had only been a minute.

"I am too sensitive," I breathed, my palm brushing over his arm and retrieving it from the bath.

He noticed the lack of my touch on his arm, which he had gladly allowed me to hold when he was fucking me with his fingers. I had to close my hands into a fist and stop myself from grabbing him by his neck and kissing him again. I missed the way his warm skin felt underneath my palm, the way muscles on his arm moved when he pushed his fingers inside me.

I eyed his stiffened dick and said, "What about you? I want to—"

"Maybe some other time," Zain said, tilting his head as he stood up, looming over the bath. "Come on, the water has turned cold. I don't want my fiancée to get sick."

Fiancée.

My mouth parted, and before I could process what he had said, I followed his lead. I bit my lip at the sight of his dripping naked body, watching his muscles move and tense as he dried himself, wrapping a towel around his waist. He helped me up from the bath, my palm holding his large, calloused hand. His eyes didn't waver from my face when water dripped down my bare body.

"Fiancée?" I managed to utter. "Since when?"

Holding a clean white towel, he said, "Since you climaxed in my hand and I had the taste of the sweetest sin." His eyes darkened, lowering down my body, my belly tightening, curling at his scorching gaze.

"I didn't know Sultan could be so crude with his words," I said, my voice small.

I hated how his voice affected me. How his coal eyes made a liquid fire pool between my legs. How his beautifully rugged face made me want to wish I could see him between my thighs. I hated how *he* affected me. I had never felt such utter lack of control when I was with someone else.

It was scary and thrilling.

Zain tsked at me, taking a step closer and patting my wet body with the dry towel as if we were having a casual conversation about the weather. "Only with you, my sweet wife," he crooned, his warm breath brushing my cheek.

I swallowed the lump in my throat when he, the Sultan of Azmia, bent on his knees wearing nothing but a towel while I stood naked, dripping with water. I gazed at his dark hair when he patted my skin dry, my legs, my thighs, my butt.

"I can do it myself, you know," I said, a flush creeping up my neck.

"I know." He gazed up at me from his knees, his face close to my heated sex. "But I wanted an excuse to touch you again."

My heart thundered when I said, "You don't need an excuse to touch me, Zain."

His lips parted, my eyes falling on them, and I had the sudden urge to hold his hair and kiss him—

Someone knocked on the door of the room, breaking the sexual pull between us. He straightened up, letting me drape the towel around me. We gazed at each other for a moment, waiting for the other to say something.

But Zain stepped out of the bathroom, giving me privacy while he went to check who was at the door with his clothes in hand.

I clutched the towel to my chest and stared at my reflection in the mirror. My dusky skin was glowing, flushed from neck to cheeks and ears. I shook my head and exhaled a sharp breath. I had to remind myself that the marriage was not based on the love that my mother wanted for me, even though we had a physical pull towards each other.

But that physical pull... it made me want to sigh, remembering how I had just orgasmed a few moments ago. His filthy words ringing in my ears, his burning eyes. I wondered what would have happened if we hadn't been interrupted. If we had landed in the sheets, kissing each other, devouring each other. I wanted to know how he would look hovering above me, how he would feel stretching me, filling me.

I wanted a round two of that night with him.

I blushed, thinking about the bulge in his pants I had seen earlier while he was busy pleasuring me.

"Nasrin?" The man of my dirty daydream knocked on the door, his eyebrow raised as he looked at me.

"Yes?" I said, my voice high-pitched.

"We are getting engaged today."

♛

"THIS IS MY YOUNGER BROTHER, KHALID," ZAIN FORMALLY introduced me to his younger brother, Prince of Azmia, who smiled at me with a small bow.

We were greeting and introducing each other to our families. My younger and older brother stayed in Maahnoor, taking care of the duties while my father and eldest brother, Sadiq Elbaz, Sultan of Maahnoor, were in Azmia.

"Where is Zara?" Zain asked a worried guard, whispering something in his ear that made his jaw clench. I wanted to ask him if his sister was okay when he smiled at my family. "My little sister will join us for lunch."

I was excited to meet Princess Zara Al Latif. She had been sheltered within Azmia and the palace so that no one but her family, the royal guards and other royals knew what she looked like. As she was the youngest Al Latif sibling and the only princess, both the brothers had kept her hidden in the palace. It was rumored that Zain didn't allow her photograph to be taken or let other people see her because she was born scarred. Or… ugly.

I didn't believe those rumors. I knew she was his half-sister, born from his second mother, but she must be a beauty, having Al Latif's genes. Zain had mentioned to me that even though he and Khalid didn't want others to see their little sister, it was her choice to keep her privacy. Her face to herself.

My father laughed. "No worries, Sultan. We are all eager to meet the Princess, especially Sadiq."

Sadiq nodded lazily, my hand finding Zain's and squeezing his hand, knowing well what my father meant. Of course, he would think of that. Marry Sadiq to the young princess who had just turned nineteen. It shamed me he would ever think about that. Sadiq was fifteen years older than her.

"Maybe she will have lunch alone." Khalid glared at my

eldest brother and my father. "Sadiq? I would suggest you erase your thoughts of marrying my sister. It will not happen as long as I am alive."

"It's Sultan Sadiq to you, Prince," he replied, gritting his teeth.

Khalid ran his eyes over my brother's form, chuckling at him, "If you truly were a sultan, Sadiq, you wouldn't have to announce it every two seconds."

I did not plan to have bloodshed on my engagement.

We hadn't exchanged the rings yet.

I cleared my throat. "I think that's enough, Prince Khalid and Brother."

Zain continued, "Lunch must be ready. Come now, let's celebrate."

Sitting beside Zain while we had our lunch at the low table with our family members was a unique experience. My father and brothers never let me sit at the head of the table. But during lunch, Zain and I sat side by side while Zara, his sweet little sister, sat at the head of the table with Khalid beside her. My brother Sadiq sat on Zara's opposite on the far end.

It was a surprise to see Princess Zara for the first time and greeting her when she gave me a dimpled smile, telling me she loved how I did my hair and needed me to teach her. I promised I would.

But knowing the angered look on Khalid's face at my father's hint of marriage, I knew there was something more than just brotherly protection towards Zara.

My father was giving Zara odd looks as she talked and laughed with Khalid, her beauty different from ours, with her pale skin, doe eyes and elfish face. I had the urge to protect her from him and Sadiq, who kept glaring at her.

I flickered my eyes from my brother to Zain's. "I should thank you for your proposal."

"And I should thank you for accepting it."

I tugged at his suit and leaned closer to whisper in his ear. "I mean it, Sultan Zain. I owe you."

He chuckled, his eyes glittering brightly. "You owe me nothing, Princess Nasrin. Let's eat before the food gets cold and tell me about your favorite sweet."

I talked to him about the sweet taste of *kunafah*, my mouth watering while I ate the spicy curry with naan. He seemed amused by my explanation and promised to try it as we talked back and forth until my father cleared his throat. For the umpteenth time.

"Here," Zain leaned over and poured water in my father's glass. "Cold water will help with the spicy food."

I tried to hide my smile and stared wide-eyed at Zara when she let out a small giggle.

My father looked furious, ignoring the glass of water. "I think it's time we discuss the marriage arrangements."

"We should. I think it'd be best if we do it early. Next month?"

Sadiq butted in, "No need to be eager, Sultan Zain. I was hoping we could wait till winter."

I certainly did not want to wait for six months and live in Maahnoor with my father and brothers.

"Why not ask Princess Nasrin?" Zara spoke up, sensing my discomfort. All heads turned towards me. "She is the bride after all."

Zain squeezed my hand and whispered, "What do you want, Nasrin?"

My stomach coiled tightly when he gazed at me with his obsidian eyes. His large hand was warm and the way his thumb caressed the pulse of my wrist made me remember that his thumb was between my legs, teasing the pulsing nub in the same manner. His eyes gleamed as if he knew what I was thinking about.

"I was thinking next week," I grinned, hoping no one could see my flush. "I can't wait to be a sultana after all."

A few of Zain's peers chuckled along with his grandma, who smiled at me. Zain squeezed my hand in return. He glanced at Sadiq. "You heard your sister. The preparation will take no longer than a few days and we will hold the wedding in the palace so you don't have to worry about the details."

"Sultan, may I suggest you exchange the rings tonight for public announcement," his advisor spoke up.

"Of course, Rahim," Sultan of Azmia looked at me. "We will have the ring ceremony this evening. If it's no trouble, I would like Nasrin to stay here, get used to being a sultana."

My brother didn't like that idea, glaring at me as I stared straight into his eyes, challenging him, daring him to belittle me. But he couldn't.

"I think that's a great idea," I said, faking a cough. "I get sick when I travel so I'll stay in Azmia."

My father rolled his eyes at my lie and continued to talk about the bonding between Azmia and Maahnoor through our marriage. How it would end the rivalry between the two countries and benefit both of them.

Zain held my hand under the table during the remainder of lunch and I missed the warmth of it when we had to stand up and go our separate ways.

16

ZAIN

"You can exchange the rings now," our advisor announced, people clapping and cheering around us.

We had finished the *tulba* ceremony privately, where I had to formally ask Nasrin's family and her for her hand in marriage. After accepting the blessings from both of our families, Rahim had announced that the royal guests had arrived to take part in our engagement.

Taking a deep breath, I held her hand and hesitated only for a moment before sliding the emerald diamond ring on her finger. Cheers erupted around us as my eyes flickered to her honeyed orbs. They were glittering when they glanced from the ring to my face.

I could imagine how she was going to complain that it wasn't something she deserved. Too bad that I was already thinking about how I would make her say 'I deserve it' with my mouth covering her soaking pussy.

I had given her a small tour of the palace that evening, showing her all the ancient riches we possessed, along with the sterling diamond ring with emerald stone she wore on her finger. It was never worn once. A heritage my mothers passed to us, making sure it was taken care of.

I knew in my heart when she smiled at the ring and asked, 'What will we have for dinner?' that it would be well taken care of on her finger, my soon-to-be-wife, Nasrin.

She took my hand, her eyes wide when she saw my palm was shaking. I cleared my throat. Biting her lip, she slid the golden band around my finger. It had a similar emerald but smaller than the diamond donning her finger. Her soft hand enveloped mine as more cheers erupted around us, glasses filled with alcohol clinking.

"Are you okay?" Nasrin asked when the photographer asked us to stand closer to each other. He gave us a forced smile and told me to wrap my hand around her waist and look thrilled.

"I am fine."

"Your hands are shaking."

"Hmm." I grunted.

"Are you regretting your decision to marry me?" she asked, peering up at me. When I didn't reply, she said, "I promise not to snore too loudly when we share a room, Sultan."

I managed to crack a smile and shook my head at her when other members of royalty surrounded us, asking us how we met, about the wedding arrangements, and how beautiful our babies would look.

Hearing the last question made me pick up a couple of glasses of champagne to cool down my warming face. I didn't understand why I was nervous and why I felt embarrassed talking about babies.

I didn't sleep well that night, being ashamed in the morning meeting with Rahim and my good friend Zayed, because I couldn't focus. I had delved deep into reading about sex late at night, trying my best to avoid watching porn and ignoring the bulge when I had imagined doing all those things with Nasrin. I couldn't seem to forget the sight of her when she had reached her peak, falling over the edge when my fingers caressed the innermost sensitive parts of her.

I was growing restless. Knowing she was staying under the same roof of the palace made me want to stalk into her room and demand to know what she had done to me. I was being foolish, acting like an imbecile since the day we got engaged. Since the day we met.

I was walking down the hallway alone, grumbling under my breath, when I found out that Nasrin had gone to visit the market with two guards. I sent four more for her protection and knew we would have a chat about it when she returned.

When I looked up, I saw Zara walking towards me, her eyes blurred with tears as her face scrunched angrily.

How dare someone—

"Zara?" I asked softly. "What happened, Princess?"

She glared at me. "Don't call me *that*."

My sister looked at me as if I had called her a rat instead of a princess.

I raised my brows, walking with her as she stomped away. "Did Khalid say something?"

She shook her head and threw her hands in the air. "Why are boys so stupid and confusing?"

"Excuse me?"

"Yes. They are. Not even boys, men are! I hate them!" She complained, shutting herself in her room before I could follow her and ask her what happened. I needed to know why my sister was complaining about boys.

"Have you seen her with someone?" I asked her guard, who was sweating. "A boy, perhaps?"

He stuttered, "N-no, Sultan."

I hummed and narrowed my eyes at him. "If she does, you will come straight to me."

He dipped his chin.

"*Say* you will."

"Y-yes, Sultan!"

"Good."

♔

"YOU ARE GETTING MARRIED TODAY, THEN WHY SUCH A LONG face?"

I averted my eyes from the window to Zayed as he entered my room. The room, which I would share with Nasrin in a few hours.

Fuck.

"I am fine, and I do not have a long face. I have a perfectly fine face of the Sultan who is getting married in an hour."

It had been a week, and all the arrangements for our wedding had been done. *Henna* that had happened last night was done peacefully, until my grandmother decided it would be a fun idea to allow the guests in the swimming pool. It had been a hassle for our staff and security team to get all the royals out from the large pool and get it cleaned before the wedding. Thankfully, Nasrin and Zara enjoyed the scene.

Zayed smiled, a dimple poking his cheek. Making himself comfortable in the armchair, eating grapes from the fruit basket, he drawled, "You are a worse liar than Khalid. You should learn from your sister."

I narrowed my eyes at him. "Has Zara been lying to you?"

Zayed grumbled, "She wins every round of poker, and she just turned nineteen. That mischievous little princess."

I chuckled, staring at such a powerful sheikh grumbling about my little sister. "We both warned you not to play against her. She has been winning against me and Khalid since she was twelve."

"It would be hard to find a decent match for her, don't you think?" Zayed raised his brow.

I sighed, already hating the idea of her growing up and finding a lover. But eventually she would grow up and find someone to spend her life with.

"I dread to even think about it. Has it been that long?"

Zayed nodded and looked at the bed covered in rose petals. I had dismissed the maids, but they said that my grandma had ordered them. It would make Nasrin feel more welcomed, they said. Knowing her, she would stroll in and fall into the bed, calling it a night while I grew restless from nervousness beside her.

He wriggled his eyebrows at me, "You should have used my oasis for your honeymoon."

I threw a grape at him, his smirk widening when he caught it in his mouth. "Just because I am getting married doesn't mean I will have sex. Here or at your oasis, which I already declined."

"Suit yourself. The offer will always stand for you and Nasrin." He asked, "So you won't have heirs? Leaving that to Khalid? Knowing him, he will never marry."

I laughed, imagining how sour Khalid's face would look if he ever heard his friend talking about him having kids. "Even I said that a few months ago and look at me. He will find his match like I did. So will Zara, and you as well, Zayed. It's inevitable."

He raked his hand through his curly dark locks. "We shall see, Sultan."

We shall.

My steps grew heavy when I entered the Court Room that had been converted into a glorious golden, white, and beige decorated room. On the dais, a similar throne was placed beside mine where Nasrin and I would sit beside each other for our *katb Al-kitaab,* which would be an official marriage ceremony. A *Qazi* (Islamic judge) would lay out the marriage conditions and rules, and if both of us agreed, including our families, we would sign the contract and be announced officially married.

Seeing so many royal guests greet and hug me with security and guards flanking me made me want to run away and hide myself somewhere. None of them were present when I was crowned a sultan at such a young age. It felt surreal and scary. I had never expected that I would get married.

"Do you need some—"

I halted Khalid's question with a shake of my head. "No. No alcohol for me right now. Is everything okay with her?"

He shrugged, his tailor-made tunic similar to mine. "Zara and grandma are with her so I wouldn't worry."

"If *jadati's* there, then I am definitely worried."

Khalid glanced at me, his dark brown eyes roving over me. "You are nervous." I huffed. He continued, "Good. If you weren't, I would have spilled this drink on you."

I cracked a small smile. He would do it in a heartbeat if I wasn't serious about my marriage with Nasrin.

The classical heady music started playing by the musicians as all the guests were informed to sit in the chairs assigned to them. I hadn't allowed the media to enter the palace, but I knew they stood waiting outside in the heat, waiting for the Sultan and Sultana to greet them from the roof. Khalid and Zayed followed me to the steps of the dais where I stood waiting for Nasrin to walk towards me.

"Are you ready, brother?"

I shook my head. "Yes."

17

NASRIN

"You look beautiful, Nasrin," Zain's grandmother cooed when Zara, dressed in a gorgeous red gown, draped a golden colored lace over my head, my dainty gold earrings glinting in the sunlight.

"You look like a queen," Zara smiled brightly, the staff asking to take pictures with me. Zara frowned at them when she asked what #SultanRoyalWedding meant.

I had forgotten that she had never used social media in her life.

"Thank you, *jadati*. Thank you, Zara. I am excited for the cake more than the wedding," I grinned, my stomach tight with the anticipation of marrying the Sultan of Azmia.

The wedding gown, jewelry, my clothes, handbags, shoes and absolutely everything else had been bought and gifted to me by Zain and his family as a part of our marriage ceremony *mahr*, which we would sign during *katb Al-kitaab*. It was a small ceremony of the payment which the groom must provide to the bride, out of love and respect.

I tried to ignore all the luxuries that came with being Zain's wife-to-be, because I could never get accustomed to seeing so many zeroes after a number in my bank account. He didn't have to do any of that, but he had promised and argued with me that if I ever wanted to separate from him in the future, it would make him feel better if I had the means to take care of myself.

Yes, Zain was utterly stupid. *Why would I ever divorce him after seeing how much he values me?*

The staff helped pin the short veil as I counted to ten, staring at my reflection. The beige color of the gown looked stunning on me. Minor details of embroidery and lace covered the delicate gown. It fit me like a second skin, cinched around the waist and flowed down to my ankles. I wasn't wearing my mother's *maang tikka,* but I had it with me in the small stitched pocket of the gown. It would be with me when I got married, almost fulfilling my mother's promise.

Zara was right. I looked like a queen with kohl eyes. But I was a nervous mess on the inside. I would share his bed. Again.

"Come now, Nasrin. Sultan is waiting for you."

My feet were light when we walked towards the beautiful dais, covered in flowers and golden fabrics. My dad was looking anywhere but at me as he held my arm for the sake of walking me towards the dais. The small crowd stood up, cheering for me, when the music intensified in the background. Through the cheers, I could feel everyone's eyes on me.

"That is going to be his wife. Ugh."

"With hips like hers, I could see why he would choose her. Heck, I want her number—"

"Isn't that the Princess of Maahnoor? He is marrying his enemy's daughter?"

"Will she be a good sultana?"

"I bet they will last a year at most."

"I think they will have a kid before the year ends."

My face flamed hearing all the words, the hold of my father's hand tightening for a moment. "Raise your chin, Nasrin. You are going to be a sultana in a few moments. Their words shouldn't matter to you," he whispered in his raspy voice.

For the first time in years, he had called me by my name with the same gentleness that I craved from a father. I reined in my shock at his words and raised my chin. Even though I could feel them sizing me up, I followed my father's words for the last time.

Then I laid my eyes on him. Every doubt and nervousness vanished. Zain looked like a dark king wearing a traditional black long tunic that reached the knees with golden thread embroidered around the cuffs and collars. He looked like a regal ruler with a small golden sheath of sword wrapped around his shoulder to waist, the white hilt of sword's handle peeking out. His brilliant hazel eyes swirled with various emotions when he gave me a small bow, offering me his hand.

When we were close enough, he whispered, "Are you okay?"

"I am now."

♛

AFTER EXCHANGING 'I DO'S' IN FRONT OF THE *QAZI* AND THE guests, Zain and I shared a small kiss on the corner of our lips announcing we were married. My hand was clutching his tightly when the professional dancers performed belly dancing and *dabke*. The veil wasn't covering my head or face anymore since Zain had removed it to kiss me. It was an odd feeling that despite watching the joyous celebration of my wedding, all I could think about was that tiny kiss.

"What are you thinking about? I am thinking about the

delicious food. I am starving," Zain murmured, patting his stomach when the guests joined in with the dancers. I could see a blur of Zara's red dress twirling and swishing as she danced with them. I knew Zain would get a lot of proposals for her after the event.

I glanced at him, his perfectly tousled hair, his intense eyes, his half-smile. "I am thinking about the cake."

"We can sneak one into our bedroom if you want." he winked at me.

Our bedroom.

"Deal."

After brief photographs with our family, we had to sit through dinner while all the royals mingled with each other. We hadn't exchanged a single word after talking about sneaking a cake into our bedroom, and I was growing more and more nervous when the moon shone in the dark sky.

Does he want to have kinky food play sex with me? Or does he want to eat the cake with me?

"Nasrin?" Zara asked, her hazel eyes staring up at me. "Can I tell you something?"

"Of course, Zara. We are sisters now."

"I know Zain can be angry sometimes and act as a hotheaded jerk—"

I gasped at her, hiding my smile. "Zara!"

"What? You know I am telling the truth."

She was.

"Yes, go on," I said, curious at what she had to say.

"Well, I want you to know that he has a heart of gold. Both of them, Zain and Khalid. They get angry easily and you can feel free to scold them because I am tired of doing it." She had a big grin on her face as she talked about her brothers, and I knew how special they were to her as she was to them.

I tucked her hair behind her ear. "Is that it? You are giving me free rein to chastise your brothers?"

"Yes!" She nodded.

"Lord save them," Zayed muttered, offering me a glass of champagne, which I gladly took, thanking him.

I had met him during the wedding arrangements, instantly taking a liking towards his exuding charm and mischievousness in making fun of Zain and Khalid. He treated Zara like his own sister and was always polite with others, but knowing he was the friend of a prince with that handsome face, there would be no shortage of women or men for the Sheikh.

Just like the Sultan.

I swallowed the bubbly drink in one go, relishing in the slight burn. Why was I so nervous about meeting Zain tonight in our room? We had been alone in a room more than a dozen times—

Because it is my wedding night.

I looked over Zayed's shoulder when he argued with Zara where my husband stood talking and nodding at two pretty women who must be royal members. They both were laughing at something he must have said. I quickly looked away when he averted his eyes to me.

My fists clenched tightly. *Why was I jealous?* I shouldn't be jealous if the Sultan was talking to two royal women. He was my husband, after all. He had promised to stay monogamous throughout our marriage.

Not if he gets bored with me first.

With that silly, bitter thought, I excused myself and asked his grandma if I could retire early, to which she winked at me. I rushed to the room on my own, asking the maids to enjoy the feast.

I held my breath, pushing open the doors of the room that I would share with Zain. Exhaling sharply, I stared in awe at the beautiful golden gossamer fabric floating around the bed in an arched shape that made the bed look like a small golden world of soft pillows and sheets. It was breathtaking. The rose petals covering the dark sheets of the enormous bed with the candles burning on the nightstand emitting an exotic scent.

Taking a shaky breath, I wandered around, noticing it was similar to my guest room, but with more space for two people. Not big enough to hide somewhere unless it was a closet or the bathroom.

Walking up to the dresser, I stared at my flushed reflection and started removing the jewelry. The emerald diamond gleamed in the dim light, making my stomach churn.

There was a knock on the door, and I tensed up. "Enter."

Zain Al Latif prowled into the room, his dark eyes pinned on me when he removed the heavily embroidered tunic, leaving him in a thin linen white shirt and pants. He eyed me warily and gently placed the small three tier cake on the table.

Aw, he kept his promise.

"Are you okay?"

I hummed and hissed when something on my hand got stuck in my hair. I tried to remove it, tugging it slowly, but it wouldn't budge.

"I guess not," I heard Zain mutter, walking towards me. His big hands wrapped around mine. "Don't be so harsh, you'll hurt yourself. Let me see."

I swallowed the lump in my throat at his closeness, his musky male cologne wafting in my brain, making me heady. His fingers felt so nice, being gentle and slow. His handsome face was focused on the task, his eyes not peering anywhere else.

"Thank you," I whispered when he was done. I looked at

him through the mirror and asked, "Can you help me with the dress?"

He nodded, clenching his jaw. I held my breath when he towered behind me, his stance powerful when he raked his hand through the loose, dark waves. I loved how his warm fingers felt when they brushed over my skin. I bit my lip, our eyes meeting briefly in the mirror before looking away.

The tension hovered between the two of us when he tugged the bow string from my back. I closed my eyes, anticipating what he would do next—

"You should go take a bath," Zain said in a clipped voice, stepping back and looking away with a light flush creeping up his neck.

Wait.

He didn't even try to seduce me or even touch me. I know he agreed not to touch me without my consent. Then why was I feeling disappointed he kept his word?

Shutting myself in the bathroom, I stripped out of the clothes and wrinkled my nose. I didn't smell bad, did I? I didn't think so. Then why did he ask me to take a bath?

Maybe to relax myself after such a long day? I tried not to overthink soaking myself in the warm bath, ignoring the disappointment of Zain, my husband, not touching me.

PART III

"Then how should I treat my wife, Sultana?"

18

ZAIN

Fuck. Fuck. Fuck.

I groaned seeing the tent in my pants and forced myself to think about anything else but Nasrin. How stunning she looked, how sweet her smile was, or the softness of her skin and the way her hair—

No, no, no, Zain.

Taking a deep breath, I eyed the closed door of the bathroom and averted my attention to the bed covered in rose petals and the gossamer golden fabric. She didn't mention it or pay it any heed.

Should I remove it? Maybe I should. It's not like she wanted to do anything else but sleep on our wedding day. She had clarified that I shouldn't even hold her hand without her permission.

I didn't mind. I had many other things to think about and work on as a sultan and being distant from her, at least physically, shouldn't hinder our marriage arrangements.

That day in the bath was just the two of us accepting each other's conditions. In a friendly way. That's all.

I lied to myself and tried to ignore how gorgeous Nasrin

looked in nothing but a heavy beige robe wrapped around her body and her wet hair after her bath. I marched past her into the bathroom to take a quick shower. I definitely did not imagine how wonderful she would look spread out underneath me on our bed, her long dark hair fawning over the pillows and her hands clutching the sheets when I thrust—

Fucking hell, Zain. I needed to get a grip on myself.

Not the literal grip.

Pretending that I had not touched myself and climaxed with filthy thoughts of her was harder than I thought. With no pun intended. She kept glancing at me when she brushed her hair, sitting on the plush stool in front of the vanity while I yanked off the bedsheet with petals on them.

"Why are you staring at me like that?" I finally asked when she stood up, dressed in a golden nightgown that cinched over her waist and flared over her hips. I had held those hips, watched them ride over my hand—

"Why did you remove the petals?"

"You certainly don't mean that you want to sleep on them." I raised my eyebrow at her little frown. "What is it you are really thinking about, Nasrin?"

She sat down on the bed, her eyes looking anywhere but at me. "I was just thinking…"

"I am terrified."

Her brown eyes narrowed at me while I tried to hide my smile and chuckled when she threw a pillow at my face. "Is that how you treat your wife, Sultan?" She mocked me in a playful tone.

Sitting down on the other side of the bed, with a lot of space between us, I asked, "Then how should I treat my wife, Sultana?"

I didn't mean to suggest seducing her, but the way her eyes lit up, I knew she understood.

"You should… you should have…" Nasrin's words stuttered, echoing in the room.

I leaned on my hands, my eyes pinned on hers. I whispered, "I should have what, my wife?"

She swallowed, my eyes fleeting to the bob of her throat on her slender neck. I resisted the urge to lean closer and lick the soft skin. "You should have tried to kiss me. We are married and…"

My eyes widened hearing her words. "Kiss you? You asked—*no*, you ordered me not to touch you."

Her frown deepened. "Well, you could have asked me if you wanted to… or not. It doesn't matter. I am exhausted."

I was confused by her behavior. She wanted me to kiss her? But she was exhausted and sleepy—

"Do you seriously think that these pillows will stop me from touching you?" I deadpanned at the trail of the pillows in the center of the bed.

Nasrin rolled her eyes. "No, Sultan. These pillows are for both of us. Do not cross them or I will…"

I smirked, "You will?"

"I will challenge you to a duel."

"You know how to wield a sword?"

"You learn a thing or two when you have three brothers."

I suppose that was true. Even Zara knew the basics of fighting, which we taught her for her own protection.

She slid under the blankets. The pillows separating us. I followed along, staring at the center of the golden fabric, and asked, "What else do you enjoy?"

"I enjoy horse riding and cooking. I make the world's best *kunafah*," she said proudly, her eyes bright when she smiled at me. She had told me it was her favorite sweet.

"Will you cook *kunafah* for me?"

"Only if you behave."

I flicked her forehead. "You are being mean. Depraving the Sultan of Azmia from the world's best *kunafah*."

She touched her forehead and scoffed, "You will not die if you don't have my *kunafah*, Zain."

I whispered to myself, "I might as well."

Before I could ask her more about her interests, I noticed she had fallen asleep. Her face so serene and calm as she slept peacefully beside me. I played with the ends of her long hair and remembered to take her horse riding the next evening.

And maybe resolve her complaint of not kissing her.

♛

I SIGHED AND GRABBED THE SOFT SKIN TIGHTER, MY HANDS trailing over the warm body, pulling it closer. I smiled to myself, burying my nose in the sweet scent of jasmine.

Wait… jasmine? Warm body? Soft skin?

My eyes opened and landed on the person sleeping beside me. Nasrin. My cheeks heated when the warm sunlight fell on her sleeping body, caressing her bare, glowing, tanned skin.

My hands were wrapped around her, her body pressed against my front. She seemed so peaceful sleeping like that in my arms, her breathing even and her long lashes creating shadows on her cheeks. I tucked a stray piece of her hair behind her ear, wishing I could kiss her cheek.

Not wanting to hear her complain about me touching her, I pulled back the pillows in array around the bed. Her hand sought me out, curling around my shoulder and pulling her closer as she hid her face on my chest.

She grumbled in her sleep, "Don't move."

I hid my smile and ran my hand through her hair. Even in her sleep, she was bossy. Leaning closer to her, I whispered, "Seducing me already, wife?"

Nasrin stirred, her eyes blinking open in confusion and watching me before she realized how she was holding onto me. Her cheeks flushed as she pulled back. "W-why were you touching me like that? What happened to the pillows… *oh*."

She looked at the pillows around us and bit back her retort. I smiled lazily. Seeing her flustered was always an endearing sight.

"You were wrapped around me like a leech, Your Grace," I mocked. "I should ask you for your intentions, but the way you were holding onto me… they seemed—"

"Stop," she said and sat up on the bed, her long black hair shining in the sunlight streaming on the bed. "It was not like that. I was just snuggling with you."

I pulled her closer by her arm, her pupils dilating when I pushed her back to my front. Pressing my body to hers, I whispered, "Like this, Nasrin?"

She nodded weakly. A gasp ricocheted in the room when I pushed my hips against hers, holding her waist and caressing the soft skin. Her hand was clutching the sheets when I slowly moved my hips back and forth, wanting her to know what she did to me.

"What are you doing, Sultan?" she gasped, her nails digging into my forearm when she felt my stiffened member pressing against her.

My warm breath caressed her neck when I kissed her skin. "Showing you what you did to me by snuggling with me."

Nasrin gasped with a small moan. The sweet sound falling off her lips made me groan, my hips thrusting harder. My grip was so tight on her waist that I prayed I wouldn't bruise her.

She twisted her body, her eyes bright in the morning sunlight. "I… I want to help you," she whispered, her voice barely audible.

"Help me?"

Her chin dipped, her eyes flickering from my hips to my face. With a flush on her cheeks, she said, "I want to return the favor, Zain."

I must have been too sleepy to stop her when she straddled me, her lips landing on the base of my throat. I sighed underneath her, closing my eyes to control myself from stripping her and entering inside her in one thrust.

Her lips lowered to my chest, her fingers scratching the hard planes of my stomach, my eyes lowering to the beautiful sight of her breasts swaying in the nightgown. Her hair tickled my skin when her kisses lowered to my hips.

I leaned up, cupping her cheek and bringing her lips to mine and kissing her. I wasn't surprised by the way Nasrin pressed closer, kissing me deeper. I growled when she bit my bottom lip, licking it. I had to pull away and look at her. Her eyes were a darker shade of brown, almost onyx, as her hand lowered inside my boxers, softly caressing my hardened veiny shaft while looking at me.

I took a deep breath in. The new sensation of her soft hand touching me felt incredible. "You know you don't have to return any favors, Nasrin," I said, my voice low and thick.

"I know," she said, kissing me once more. "But I want to please you, Your Grace."

She leaned down my spread legs, removing the boxers with her slender fingers. My cheeks flushed hearing the small gasp from her lips when she came face to face with my cock. I had precum glistening on the tip. Her eyes flickered to my face for a moment before lowering to my shaft.

I bit my lip, watching her fingers wrap around me with half-lidded eyes. Her other hand caressed my thigh as she stroked me, squeezing at the base in a way that made me groan. I had never felt such pleasure before. I had when I made her come, but not like that, the way a shiver curled down my body.

My muscles tightened when her lush mouth lowered to the tip, licking the precum with the tip of her pink tongue before sucking it in her mouth. I closed my eyes, clenching the sheets in my hand when Nasrin sucked me again, a throaty groan escaping my lips.

I parted my lids and watched her lower her lips on me, my cock sliding inside her warm and wet mouth, making me curse. Her cheeks hollowed as she pleasured me with her sinful mouth, my hips straining not to thrust inside her. I didn't want to hurt her.

"If you keep doing that," I breathed. "I will cum inside your mouth, Nasrin."

She pulled away, a string of saliva following her as she licked her lips. "Do as you please, Sultan," she said in her husky voice, while smiling.

She fucking smiled.

I couldn't stop myself from wrapping my hand around her hair and tugging her towards me and kissing her pillowy lips. She moaned into my mouth when I deepened the kiss, letting her know how much her words aroused me.

"You wreck me, Nasrin," I whispered, pulling away and glared at her. "Don't say things like that unless you are asking to be fucked until you can't walk properly for a week."

Her cheeks reddened, her eyes darkening as she licked her lips. "What if I am asking just that?"

I shook my head at her in disbelief. "I won't be gentle," I warned when she lowered herself in front of me again, the bed dipping once again, the slit on her nightgown revealing the delicious dusky golden skin of her thighs.

"I don't mind," she said, her warm breath caressing my sensitive shaft. I clenched my jaw when she took me in her mouth once again, my fingers digging on her scalp as my climax grew closer and closer.

I held her hair, caressing her hollowed cheeks when I filled her. "Stop me if it hurts, Nasrin."

Her eyes met mine as I thrust inside her welcoming mouth, watching them get wide. I stayed still, my breathing harsh. I slowly slid out and repeated my actions. Her fingers dug into my inner thigh, her legs squirming as the sounds of my low groans echoed in the room.

Nasrin moaned when I fucked her mouth, the reverberations tightening my balls as I peaked over my edge. I warned her before sliding my entire length inside her and groaned, releasing thick spurts of my seed inside her mouth.

I licked my lips, watching her neck bob as she swallowed, my heart thundering in my ears. She pulled back to lick at the veins of my shaft.

I sighed and fell back on the bed, muttering, "You truly wreck me."

Nasrin straddled me, her face flushed and hair tousled. "Was that too much for the sultan of such a powerful country?" She teased with a grin, having no right to be so beautiful after doing… what she did moments ago.

I glided my hands over the soft skin of her thighs. "It was. I have never felt that way before. Thank you."

She frowned. "You don't have to thank me, Zain. Was it truly that good of a blow—?"

"Sultan!"

I made a sound of complaint, hearing the guard at our door knocking and calling me. I had to ignore the small whine Nasrin made when I pulled away from her, apologizing for the disturbance, and wore my dark robe from the armchair.

Making sure I looked decent, I unlocked the door and

glared at the guard. "What was so important that you had to wake me—"

"It's your siblings, Sultan. Prince Khalid asked for you and to tell you it's urgent. Something about Princess Zara."

He didn't have to tell me twice.

"I will meet them in her room in a few minutes," I said, and closed the door.

Nasrin was standing by the bed, a frown marring her gorgeous face, her nightgown in disarray. "Did something happen? Is Zara in any trouble?"

"When is she not in trouble, Nasrin," I sighed and smiled at the thought of my little sister causing trouble wherever she goes. "She has been a tiny rebel ever since our father died. Going horse riding alone in a desert with no guards, painting with Khalid when she should be studying with her tutor, pranking Zayed, knowing full well that he is a sheikh."

I shook my head and buttoned my shirt, "We have tried so hard to protect her, but she can't stay long without causing some trouble."

Nasrin walked towards me, straightening the collars of my shirt. I tried to keep my heart steady when she smiled at me. "Let her be, Zain. She is a teenager and she should have a little fun. She is kind, and I have seen her threaten a guard and he looked ready to piss his pants, so I am sure she can protect herself."

"I know she can," I said, thinking about the past. My cruel father. The night he died. "But that doesn't mean we will ever stop worrying about her."

I kissed her forehead. "I am not sure when I will be back. Get some rest and eat the cake. Don't make any plans for this evening."

"Why?"

I paused at the door and looking over my shoulder, I answered, "I am taking you out, wife."

Her eyes sparkled. I didn't know I was smiling when I entered the usual bubbly room of Zara, the gloomy atmosphere wiping the smile off of my face. She was sitting on her bed while Khalid was standing near the window, his posture stern.

What the hell happened here?

19

NASRIN

It seemed like the memories of his warm body around me had burned in my mind. I couldn't stop thinking about that morning, the way I had been so flustered and aroused. His grip on my waist was strong, his thrusts powerful when they rubbed over me, making me ache for him, his words dirty but his voice velvety smooth.

That was one thing, but the way he had reacted to my touch... that had been one of the most erotic sights I had ever seen. Zain Al Latif loved to be vocal when he was on the receiving end of oral sex. The thrill of sucking him and taking him in my mouth was something I had never experienced before. It had aroused me. Pleasuring and pleasing him had aroused me.

I wanted to whine when he had to leave, wanting to wrap myself around him once again and make him release inside me.

It was absurd. How badly I wanted him to fuck me.

Shaking my head at my impure thoughts, I stepped out of the bathroom and got ready for my first day as the Sultana of Azmia. I had breakfast with the family, but Zara was absent from the table. Both Khalid and Zain glared at their plates. Even Grandma couldn't make them break out of their silent anger. Something must have happened when Sultan had to leave early in the morning to check up on her.

Was she okay? If she wasn't, he would have told me, but he wouldn't even look at me. I would need to check up on her as soon as I could.

I was led to Sultan's study, an enormous room with floor to ceiling bookshelves and a mahogany desk with papers and documents atop it. A balcony overlooked the beautiful city shining like gold in the sunlight.

"Nasrin." I turned around to see Zain, his hair slicked back in a rough tousle. He looked as sharp as ever in a dark suit. "What are you doing here?"

I swallowed the lump in my throat, remembering about that morning, how flushed his cheeks had turned after releasing inside my mouth, the gentle caress of his hands on my thighs.

"I wanted to see where you work. Would I have my space like this for being a sultana?"

"If you want, I will get it arranged, but you don't need to worry about handling everything like a sultana. I will ask you only when I need your help."

I sighed, trailing my finger on the mahogany desk. "That's no fun."

"I thought you wanted to work as a vet?" he asked, placing his suit jacket over his chair and sitting on the seat, rolling his sleeves over his arms. My throat went dry at the sight of his arms.

I must have not slept well if I was getting aroused at just the sight of his arms.

"I do. I talked with Zayed as he handles our stables. I will meet the doctor at the vet clinic today," I said with a small smile on my face.

I had missed working with animals and treating them. It made my heart full to help the animals with their needs. In London, I had worked in a vet clinic, so I needed to learn about working with horses and how to treat them.

Zain tilted his head, a lock of hair falling over his forehead. "Did you have any pets growing up?"

"Other than horses, we didn't have any pets. I wanted to have a farm with chickens, horses, dogs, cats." I laughed at my childhood dream, feeling embarrassed to talk about it in front of Sultan, in front of Zain. "It was a silly childhood dream."

He seemed amused hearing my answer, "It's not sillier than mine."

"Really? What was your childhood dream?"

"I wanted to save the world, be a superhero and have a pet tiger named Teddy."

A laugh bubbled out of me, my hand clutching my stomach. My brain imagined Zain in a cape and spandex, saving the world with a tiger. I shook my head, wiping the tears from my eyes.

"Okay, you can stop laughing now," he muttered. "My heart is wounded."

I giggled, striding towards the plush chair he sat on. "I wonder how you would look in spandex."

Zain raised his eyebrow and said in a husky voice, "Don't get any naughty ideas, wife."

Wife. I loved how effortlessly that rolled off his tongue. It made my heart flip.

"I thought the Sultan of Azmia would be a little adventurous when it came to nightly physical activities," I teased.

He parted his lips to reply when someone knocked on the door of his study. Right, I had forgotten that we were in his study and he was a busy man.

"We will continue this talk of being adventurous in our

nightly physical activities later, Nasrin. Come here," he said, leaning back in the chair in a way that made my stomach dip.

When I was close within his reach, he held my arm and pulled me close enough to brush his lips against mine, kissing them. "Wear something comfortable this evening," he whispered, tucking the lock of hair behind my ear.

"Why? Are we going to be adventurous?" I asked.

Zain laughed, the husky, soft sound tickling over my cheek. I loved the sound of his laugh, the sight of his white teeth and the small crinkles of his eyes. It was so sincere and raw and adorable that I wished I could take a picture of him.

"We will be adventurous, but not in the sense you are thinking, you naughty girl." He grinned.

"You're no fun," I mocked, kissing him on the lips before pulling away. I had to turn away from him to hide the rising blush on my neck when I made my way to the door, hoping he wouldn't notice the tremble in my legs.

He had kissed me out of the blue. He was not what I had in mind for marrying the Sultan of Azmia. I had thought of the worst, about him and how he would treat me, but Zain was nothing like that. Guilt washed over me as I left the study, the guard bowing at me before he entered the room.

♔

ZARA WOULDN'T OPEN HER DOOR WHEN I WENT TO CHECK UP on her. Her maid and guards had warned me that the Princess didn't want to be disturbed, but I didn't care. I knew something had happened and wanted to make sure she was okay. Her silence meant that she was not.

I tried not to worry, knowing she would come out of her shell on her own and maybe even chastise her brothers.

I would have asked Zain what had happened, but I didn't

want to be nosy, and he was busy. Khalid, too, had shut himself in his studio to paint.

That evening, I had finished getting freshened up after spending the day in the vet clinic and was smelling like soap and baby powder when Zain entered our room. He asked me if I was ready. I tried to ignore the butterflies in my belly when he took my hand in his.

"Do you want to tell me about what happened this morning?" I asked, wanting to know about the feud between the siblings.

Zain smirked at me. "Which part, wife? The one when you snuggled up to me or when I came inside your mouth or when we were about to have se—"

My cheeks warmed, and I looked away, wishing the ground would swallow me up. "I didn't mean… *that*. I was talking about Zara."

His smirk slipped off. "Khalid found out about her sneaking away, and it was pure agony to see both of them angry with each other."

Even though Zara and Zain were close, she was closer to Khalid.

"She went out of the palace?"

Zain flickered his eyes to me and said, "Yes, on New Year's Eve, the night before her birthday. I had allowed her to go to our club with Khalid, with us, knowing well that he would keep his eyes on her and make sure she was safe. I had even doubled her security—"

"But?"

"She fooled the guards by dressing up as a maid. She went to a different club on her own."

She was smart, kind, beautiful, and cunning. Was there anything that girl couldn't do?

He squeezed my hand, "Stop smiling."

I grinned. "I am wondering how clever she is to convince

her maid to play along with it and even trick the guards. Was she safe at this other club she went to?"

Zain sighed, looking at the blue sky when we walked out of the palace. "We are not sure. She said she was safe, but that club is a tourist spot. Khalid realized she didn't once meet him at our club, so he looked for all the surveillance footage and found her talking to some… some man at the club."

Oh. I could understand why they were both mad. Being overprotective brothers, they thought some stranger had tainted their little sister.

"Was she hurt?" I asked, my voice clipped.

"No, if she was… I would have made sure he can never walk and talk again. She didn't tell us about what happened afterwards, but we both suspect what must have happened."

I held his fists, caressing the knuckles, and met his dark eyes, furious and guilty. "Give her some space and time, Zain. She is young—"

"She is nineteen. She should know better than to mingle all night with some strange man."

"*Zain*," I said. "Give her some time. She will apologize to you for sneaking out, but you need to stop restricting her to the palace. She won't grow up or get to enjoy her life if you keep her locked in these walls, no matter how beautiful it is."

"I don't keep her locked," he said. "I allow her to go out."

"With her guards," I pointed out. "Ask her if she has any friends other than the guards or maids who always surround her everywhere she goes."

Zain's silence was my answer. I kissed his knuckles and whispered, "Give her your love and the freedom she needs."

He gazed at our entwined hands and pulled me closer, wrapping his arms around me, giving me a hug. I heard him take a deep breath as I caressed his back, feeling him relax.

"I wish you had been there with me this morning. We raised our voices in front of her, Nasrin," he said, and I could hear the hurt and the guilt in his soft voice. "For the first time, we raised our voices towards our little sister and I saw how much pain we caused her. Not even listening to what she had to say."

I pulled away to look at him and saw how tired his eyes looked. It hurt me to see him that way. "Apologize when she is ready. Listen to what she has to say and then try to understand her, okay? I will be with you if you want me to."

"I would like that."

I smiled at him as he led me to the stables, my eyes trailing over the gorgeous horses, their coats shining as some of them snorted at us.

"You went to London for your degree when you were the same age as her," Zain said. "Were you like her?"

I chuckled at him and remembered my university days. "I was not a rebel like her, nor did I sneak out. I used to stay in the dorms and on the weekends we would party, get drunk and…"

"And?" he asked, raising his eyebrow.

Say it, Nasrin, he is your husband and the Sultan after all.

"And sleep around," I finished, confused by the shocked look on his face, which he quickly recovered.

"You have had lovers before," he said, more to himself than me.

"Yes, Zain." I asked, patting the muzzle of the white horse. "It doesn't bother you, does it?"

He shook his head, checking the reins and the saddle, making sure it was comfortable. "No, it doesn't bother me."

"Right, it shouldn't." I chuckled awkwardly. "I mean, you are a sultan, so you must have had many lovers as well."

Zain didn't reply.

"Zain?" I asked, peering at his face.

He held me by my hips and settled me on top of the horse, making sure I was comfortable. "I didn't have any lovers.

Other than you," he said in a clipped voice, his neck flushed when he took hold of the reins and sat behind me in one graceful sweep.

I was glad he couldn't see me because I was gaping and clutching the leather tightly after hearing his words. He didn't have any lovers? He was not someone I was imagining him to be.

But how? The way he had touched me and had sex with me that night. The way he had made me come apart in the bath, the way he had guided me over his length... I thought—

He was a virgin? The Sultan of Azmia was a virgin, and he slept with me, a stranger, that night. I couldn't wrap my head around it. Not once did I think he would be inexperienced by the way he had acted that night. I had confused his blushing and fumbling hands for excitement and nervousness. Not inexperience.

I swallowed the lump in my throat.

Oh God.

I am a terrible person to ever think that Zain was a terrible ruler like my father, a man after his own selfish needs and never once caring about me. I thought he had been with plenty of women and I was so, so wrong. He was never that. He was just Zain. My sweet, handsome and a little wild husband.

20

ZAIN

The sound of the royal horse galloping in the golden sand surrounded us. Even with the loud wind blowing against us, I could hear Nasrin thinking after knowing that I was inexperienced the night we met.

I wasn't ashamed of it, but seeing my wife tense around me made me feel embarrassed. Just for a moment, I wished I had taken heed of Khalid's advice and had some experience in pleasuring women so I could ease whatever Nasrin was overthinking about.

With a clipped voice, I told her to cover her nose when the sand of the desert started flowing with the wind. I wrapped the *keffiyeh* around my nose, covering my mouth and neck, watching Nasrin's finger fumble with the knot.

"May I?" I asked, speaking for the first time, knowing full well she was panicking over my virginity.

She nodded tersely, holding the reins and leading the horse while I gently tied the knot of the fabric, making sure her nose and mouth were covered.

Nasrin asked, "Where are we going?"

"To see the sunset," I said. "But if you want to go back, we can—"

"No, I would like to see the sunset with you, Zain."

There was gentleness in her voice despite her reaction when she came to know the truth of my sex life. Surely she must have thought of a plan in the Nasrin way. I wanted to ask her what she was thinking about. If my inexperience had embarrassed her or… surprised her.

Or something much worse?

"This is…" Nasrin started, her voice a small whisper when the horse slowed down, stopping on the top of a sand dune.

I jumped down, holding her hand and waist as I lowered her on the sand, careful not to touch her anywhere inappropriate or stare too long at her marvelous breasts. I reined in my arousal and watched how her brown eyes were bright, like molten chocolate, in awe at the view.

I was in awe, too.

How could she look more beautiful than before after riding a horse in the desert? With her ruffled hair framing her face, her wide grin at the scenery ahead of us and laughing when she brushed the horse's mane, hearing him snort again.

Swallowing the lump in my throat, I lowered my *keffiyeh* and stood beside her. Two hundred years ago, both of our families had joined to fight off the attack from our neighboring country. I could remember my father talking about the Great Sand War held in the desert where his great grandparents had fought. That we should be thankful to have Al Latif blood running in our veins.

But that was the excuse he gave himself when he wanted to teach me and Khalid a lesson, punishing us and beating us when we didn't follow in his footsteps.

"Hey…" Nasrin stood across from me, "Are you okay?"

"I was thinking about the Great Sand War."

Holding my hand in hers, she laid her head on my shoulders. I tried not to overthink about the casual gesture, similar to the kiss she had given me earlier in the study. Instead, I focused on the jasmine scent of hers, her soft breaths.

"Why are you thinking about the past, Sultan? All I see is the beautiful scenery of the setting sun, standing beside my husband."

I flickered my eyes to hers. "To know your future and be a better ruler than our ancestors, it is important to remember the past. I don't want to be like my father."

"Salman Al Latif? My father used to gloat about their friendship and looked up to him for any guidance." She squeezed my hand, noticing the hard lines on my face when she said the name of that man. I never wanted to hear her utter that name again. "Was he not a good person?"

"He was not a good person, husband or a father."

There was a silence between us that stretched for a few moments.

Nasrin said, "From how I see it, Zain, you are not at all like your father. You are a good person, even though you act cold sometimes. A good husband? Hmm, ask me about it in a week because we got married yesterday. You are a great brother to both Khalid and Zara, trying to understand them, so I can guess that you'd be a brilliant father."

I looked down at her, and she was gazing up at me with a small smile. "You think so?" I asked.

I had never thought that I was a good person or that I could be a better father than my father was. But hearing Nasrin say that to me with a proud smile made my heart thud loudly in my ears. It meant something special and precious when *she* said that.

"I know so, Sultan."

I was aware of her little palm in mine, the soft pads of her fingers caressing my knuckles. The closeness between us.

The way I felt when she stood beside me with her hair in loose tendrils and her tanned skin glowing, smiling at me with her pretty lips and brown doe eyes.

I wanted to hold her closer and kiss her. *Fuck.* I wanted to kiss her badly.

"Nasrin," I said. "I am going to kiss you."

Her eyes widened, and she nodded, a whisper of 'yes' coming out of her lips before I covered them with mine. I sighed, and she gasped at the tingle of our lips, kissing each other with gentleness and curiosity.

Everything faded but her. Her soft body pressing closer to mine, her hands tangling in my hair. The way she moaned sweetly when I pressed my hand on her lower back, urging her closer.

"Zain," she gasped.

"Nasrin," I breathed, pulling away and panting to catch my breath when she did the same. Her cheeks were flushed, her pupils dilated, and her lips… so tempting and inviting.

"Was that okay?" I heard myself ask, my voice deeper than before, my hands cupping her face, her fingers clutching my shirt tightly.

"More than okay," she replied, and leaning up on her toes, she brushed her lips over mine. Her eyes peered up at me. "Can we do that again, Sultan?"

I smiled at her. "Your wish is my command, Sultana."

We kissed again.

And some more.

I pulled her on top of me in the middle of the empty desert, the horse neighing as we laughed and kissed once again. Her hair tangled in my hands when she kissed me with sweet passion.

We had to stop because the sun had set, and the sky was slowly turning dark. I had held her close on our ride back to the palace, her hands entwined with mine when she leaned back against me.

"Why do you both look like you wrestled in the sand?" Khalid taunted when we walked hand in hand into the palace.

Our clothes were disheveled, hair mussed with sand covering us, but our faces were glowing. We must have resembled two kids who had the time of their life playing in the sand.

"Maybe we did, Khalid," Nasrin answered with her chin high. "I tackled my Sultan in the desert and won."

My Sultan.

My brother raised his eyebrow at her, giving me a look and smirking at both of us. "Sure, you did, Sultana. You have certainly made my brother speechless."

I glared at his smug smile. "Excuse us, Khalid. We need to wash off the sand and let *jadati* know we will take our dinner in our room."

"Just the dinner or tomorrow's breakfast, too?" He teased.

Nasrin was hiding her laugh when my cheeks felt warm. "Get out of my sight before I punch you, Khalid."

My wife held my hand and dragged me away from there, leaving Khalid to chuckle behind us.

"I apologize for my brother's behavior, I will scold—"

"*Zain.*" Nasrin grinned at me, "It's okay, Khalid was mocking us like all siblings do."

I nodded at her, brushing my thumb over her knuckles. We were walking back to our room when someone rushed into us.

"I am so sorry, I wasn't looking where I was going—"

Nasrin apologized quickly to the young woman with short hair...

"Zara?" I asked, bending down on my knees to look at her face. "Zara, what happened?"

Her hazel eyes were red and swollen as tears slid down her cheeks. I pulled her into a hug, squeezing my eyes shut when she sobbed into my neck, apologizing to me. I noticed she had chopped her hair off to her chin, and I knew something had happened, but I needed to make sure she was okay.

"Shh, sweetheart, it's okay. I forgive you for everything," I murmured, wiping away her tears as she heaved and drank the water that Nasrin had brought us.

"I am so sorry, Zain. I was being so stupid, sneaking away like that," Zara said, her hazel eyes on the ground. "I wanted to go out of the palace and have some fun."

I shared a look with Nasrin, begging her to help me with my eyes. Growing up, it was a rare sight to see Zara cry. Even if she fell and bruised her elbows or knees, sprained her ankle, she never cried. Just laughed it off. She only ever sobbed and cried like that once. For Khalid after he had killed our father.

"It's okay, sweet. See? Your brother forgave you. He was not mad at you for wanting to go out. We can talk about it after dinner. Until then, let me help you with your hair, okay?"

Zara looked at me and then at Nasrin. She finally nodded, "Thank you, Nasrin."

I stood up and watched Nasrin take my sister back to her room, talking to her in a soft voice. I had to find out why she was so hurt that she cut her own hair. For as long as I remember, Zara loved her long, wavy coal hair. She must have been furious and sad to chop it off.

I needed to talk to Khalid.

"Will my brothers scold me?" Zara asked, her voice small, sulking in the chair.

"For what?" I asked, watching the hairdresser snip away at her roughly cut hair.

I had called the best hairdresser in Azmia, offering a bonus if she would cut the Princess's hair in her room and keep it a secret. I was sure Zain wouldn't want rumors about Zara spreading across like a wildfire.

"For disappointing them," she answered.

"They are not disappointed in you, Zara. You are their little sister. You could never disappoint Zain or Khalid. They got a little mad because they thought they couldn't protect you, and that you are hurt because of their carelessness."

"I don't want them to be angry because of me, Nasrin," she muttered. "How do I make them not mad? Khalid won't even look at me."

Swallowing the lump in my throat, I squeezed her hand. "I asked Zain to talk to you after dinner and bring Khalid with him. You can resolve any conflict by communicating, Zara. I am sure your brothers will understand or at least try to understand and do anything to help you because they care about you."

She nodded and gave me a small smile. Even though it was not her full dimpled smile, it was still better than the frown.

The hairdresser stepped back, removing the cloth from Zara's neck and brushing away the stray hair. As Zara had chopped her hair very unevenly, the hairdresser gave her a pixie bob. Her chocolate-colored hair was slicked back and a fringe with short hair framed her elfish face, bringing out her sharp bone structure.

"Do you like it, Princess?" The hairdresser asked with a meek voice, afraid of her rejection.

Zara grinned at her and bowed her head. "I love it, thank you so much!"

I smiled at her, playing with her hair, seeing it from all the different angles. *Zara is going to break many hearts in the future.* When the hairdresser was paid in full with a tip, she left, leaving Zara and me alone in her room.

"Can I ask why you were so sad and angry that you chopped your hair?" I said.

"I wasn't angry at myself, even though I was stupid. I was angry at… at someone," she grumbled.

I hummed. "Was that someone a male?"

Zara stared at me with wide eyes. "Please don't tell my brothers or they will kill me. Or worse, they will kill him."

"They will not kill him, Zara," I chuckled. "I assure you they know even they can't protect you from love and heartbreak."

She gave me a smile and hugged me. "I am so glad you are here, Nasrin. Thank you for marrying my brother."

I was touched by her words. Hugging her back, I whispered, "I am glad too."

"Is she okay?" Zain asked me as soon as I entered the room.

His hair was damp, and he was wearing clean clothes, smelling of mint and jasmine. Did he use my body wash? It made me smile.

"She is. I promised her that you and Khalid will talk to her after dinner. Please listen to what she has to say before making any assumptions."

"I will. Did she mention what happened?"

"I believe your sister got her heart broken."

Maybe I shouldn't have said that. Maybe I should have let Zara tell him that because as soon as I finished my sentence, Zain's face turned from confused to shocked to anger.

"How dare someone break my little sister—"

I walked past him, "I shouldn't have told you."

"What do you mean? Someone had the audacity to break my sister's heart and—"

"Zain," I said. "Are you hearing yourself? Yes, you are a sultan and yes, she is the Princess of Azmia, but that doesn't mean you or Khalid could protect her from being in love, getting heartbroken and growing up."

He looked wounded and I couldn't believe my eyes. Zain was pouting. "But… she is my sister."

"And she will always be your sister, Zain. Give her the freedom and allow herself to love someone. Let her learn things on her own and maybe guide her with the heartbreak."

Zain looked at me for a moment, processing my words and nodding to himself. Averting his eyes from the floor to me, he covered the distance in a few steps and claimed my lips with his. I gasped in surprise, closing my eyes and kissing him back, his hand warm against my cheek.

"I don't know what I would do without you, Nasrin," he whispered. "Thank you."

"If she was my sister, you'd do the same, Zain. If not more. You don't need to thank me for it. You are my husband."

His coal eyes burned at hearing my words, his hand lowering to my waist, not caring that I was covered in sand. "Say that again," he commanded, his voice like velvet, making my toes curl into the Egyptian rug.

"You are my husband," I whispered.

He kissed me again, our kiss scorching, his gentle yet firm touch igniting shivers all over my body. That kiss was different from the ones we shared in the desert. They were sweet and tender. But that kiss was passionate and wild and raw.

As if he wanted to undress me right there and fuck me on the floor over the rug.

I whined when Zain pulled away. I heard the knocking on the door. He kissed the corner of my lips, "We should continue this later."

I agreed too quickly, "Yes, we should."

Zain's eyes were dark and clouded when he took a step back. "Go take a shower and I will make arrangements for our dinner."

The way he said it, I knew it was more of a command than anything. Biting my lip, I turned and rushed to the en suite bathroom to take a shower. After all, who was I to deny his majesty's command?

After getting ready in comfortable clothes and letting my wet hair loose, I stepped out to see Zain talking to someone on the phone. A vein was popping out of his neck as he paced back and forth around the room.

"Is everything okay?" I asked, peering at him when he furiously ended the call, glaring at his phone.

Zain looked at me, his furrowed brows relaxing once he saw my worried expression. "Nothing you need to worry about. Khalid is being a stubborn ass, that is all."

"Sit, let me help you with it," he said, making me sit on the stool in front of the dresser. Taking a soft towel, he gently patted my wet hair and ran a comb through it. It reminded me of the day we got engaged, how he had dried my body with a towel after the bath.

I smiled at our reflection, wondering how I could have ever thought so low of him before. He was nothing like the rumors that I had heard in Maahnoor. Zain was a stern and just ruler, but around his family, he was sweet and kind.

"Can I ask you something?"

"Ask away, Sultana."

Taking a deep breath, I said, "Why didn't you sleep with anyone? You are a sultan. I am sure you must have had lines of beautiful people wanting to warm your bed, Zain."

He met my eyes through the reflection, his jaw clenched. "I didn't care about beautiful people wanting to sleep with me. I was twenty when I became a sultan, the youngest that anyone has ever been. I had a tremendous responsibility on my shoulders and still have. I didn't think it was right for me to go to parties and have casual sex. So, I didn't."

Turning me around, he bent on his knees and held my hands, his thumb caressing the emerald ring on my left ring finger. "I vowed to myself that I wouldn't have sex until I felt confident in my position to take care of that person, whoever it may be. Sex is not something that I value and I thought I didn't care about it... until I saw you. I thought I would forget you after that night in the club, but after seeing you in the library, in the gardens, I knew I couldn't. I saw your honey eyes when you glared at me for forcing you to choose me and not that sheikh as a husband. I knew I had to marry you."

I chuckled and cupped his cheeks, the stubble grazing my palms. "That's very romantic, Sultan." He kissed my palm, and I added, "But I don't want you to feel pressured about it. I am happy and content when you are with me."

"So am I," he whispered, leaning closer to kiss me. I closed my eyes, breathing in his musky male scent, the jasmine of my body wash. He had to pull away when someone knocked on the door.

I refrained from whining, glaring at the door. Zain chuckled and tapped my nose as he stood up, "It must be our dinner."

PART IV

"Let your Sultan watch."

22
ZAIN

The atmosphere was tense, like the day before when I entered Zara's room after my dinner with Nasrin. She had told me to be good and behave. I wasn't expecting my sister smiling and talking with Khalid. Her hair was shorter than before, that suited her almost too well.

She was going to break so many hearts. I already pitied them.

After complimenting her on her new hairstyle, I asked her if she was okay. We talked about what had happened that caused all of us to be mad at each other. We both listened to her, soothing her in a calm voice when she told us about the heartbreak, some boy ghosting her.

Khalid and I shared a relieved look when she told us how angry she was at him. We knew if it had been more than that, we would have to take action. After she calmed down, I asked her what she wanted to do next. She was excellent in all her academic subjects, but we knew none of them made her want to pursue it in the future.

"I want to travel the world," she answered, her hazel eyes sparkling.

"Okay, we can help you with the—"

"All on my own."

"What?" Khalid and I said in unison. The thought of her wandering around the globe all alone made me shudder.

"Yes. I want to travel the world on my own. I want to explore unknown places, eat new cuisines, meet new people, learn new cultures and do all of that with my own money."

I shared a look with Khalid, and I knew we were both thinking the same thing as Zara talked about travelling the world with a dimpled smile.

Our sister was growing up.

♛

"Who is she talking to?" I asked, shooting daggers at the pubescent boy, who was smiling at my wife with hearts in his eyes.

Zayed chuckled beside me, "Don't tell me you are jealous of him, Zain."

"What if I am?" I grumbled, crossing my arms.

Nasrin laughed at something he said, her hand brushing over the muzzle of the horse. It had been over a week since we kissed in the desert and since then, we had been sharing a lot of kisses and cuddles while we talked about our days with each other. We hadn't explored anything other than giving and receiving oral. Just like that morning, how she had come apart on my tongue, my name rolling off of her tongue in sweet harmony.

Nasrin wanted to see Zayed's stable and spend the day in the veterinarian clinic. But that didn't mean she could show off her pretty smile like that and make me jealous—

"You are such a fool, Zain," Zayed snickered.

"I am not a fool."

"You are a lovely fool. Instead of glaring at the poor boy, just greet your wife. It's not that hard."

"Don't tell me what to do."

I stormed away, not liking the new feeling that had been churning in my heart whenever I see Nasrin. I know she is beautiful and wants the best for her city and to save animals, but that didn't mean she could do as she pleased and steal my heart too.

"I have a confession to make," I told my grandmother, who was oiling Zara's short hair and laughing with her.

Both the women looked at me with raised eyebrows.

I blurted, my cheeks red, "I think I might like Nasrin."

"About time," my grandma said while my sister laughed at me.

"Of course you do, Brother. She is your wife after all."

"No, I… it's not like that. I have never felt like this before. I don't know what to do," I said, pacing around the hallway that looked over the garden. The same garden where I had argued with Nasrin. "Even those flowers and the sun and moon remind me of her. Is this normal?"

My sister kept giggling while Grandma chuckled and asked me to lean down. She ruffled my hair and said, "You are in love, boy. Only love can turn rulers like you into a fool."

"Why does everyone keep saying that?" I grumbled, "I am not a fool."

"A handsome, lovely fool, Zain," she smiled. "When your father first saw your mother in the market, he rushed to me in the evening and announced that he was going to marry her."

Zara stopped smiling and looked away.

I clenched my fists. "I am not like him."

♛

"Zain," I heard Nasrin call out and quickly stood up, hiding my shaking hands in my pants. "Where are you?"

"I am here on the balcony," I said, looking around and making sure everything was perfect.

After my confession to Grandma and Zara, I decided to do something special and spend time with Nasrin. I had asked the cooks to make a delicious lamb steak with spiced yogurt for dinner and decorated the sitting area in the balcony of our room. The sky was turning darker, and the pool had fresh water running, which gleamed in the moonlight with candles surrounding it. The dining table was set up with all the plates and glasses with jasmine, her favorite flowers, in the middle.

I hope she likes it.

"Zain… what is all this?" She was gaping, her eyes flickering between me and her surroundings.

"I thought we could have dinner together." I scratched my neck nervously. "Why? Is something wrong? Are jasmine not your favorite flowers?"

Nasrin let out a soft chuckle, her honeyed eyes sparkling. "No, no, it's perfect." Leaning on her toes, she pressed her lips against mine. "I love it, Zain."

I love you.

I blinked at her and tried to smile when my heart thudded loudly against my ribs. I did not just think that, did I? Could it be possible for me, of all people, to be in love? With Nasrin?

"Why don't we freshen up and you can tell me all about your day. There's still some time before dinner," I said, leading her inside the room.

When she was getting ready, I changed into a crisp white shirt, pants, and suit jacket. I couldn't help but shamelessly stare at her when she stepped out onto the balcony wearing a dark satin dress that hugged her curves, accentuating them.

"You look stunning, Nasrin. Forgive me, but I don't think I will be able to keep my hands to myself tonight."

Her cheeks turned pink, tucking a loose strand of her hair behind her ear. Our knees touched as we sat on the seating of the low table. The staff served our food. Her eyes brightened when she noticed it was her favorite dish with white wine.

When they left, we started our dinner. I listened to her talk about the urgent care one dog needed and how she helped the doctor with the case. I was relieved to know that the dog would be okay and be with his owner in no time. I was proud of her work, saving animals' lives and taking care of them.

I asked her for her guidance with the women's council, asking if she would be a part of it. Her input could help make Azmia a better country for all genders.

"I tried to look for a way to dethrone Sadiq and let Imran be the Sultan of Maahnoor," I said. "But there's no way unless he rejects the crown or… dies."

Nasrin winced hearing me. I covered her hand. "I knew it wouldn't be possible. That was a silly thought."

I didn't want to see her lose hope in her own country just because Sadiq Elbaz was not the sultan that Maahnoor deserved. "You and I will make changes, Nasrin."

She smiled, her eyes soft, "I believe you, Sultan."

"I don't want to be rude, but I wanted to know why you, Zara or Khalid, act differently whenever someone mentions your father?" Nasrin asked when the maids cleared our plates after our dinner.

I took a big gulp of the white wine, knowing I needed the sweet burning taste to tell her the truth of what had happened all those years ago. She was our family. She was my family and needed to know the truth.

"When we were little, our father used to dote on me and Khalid. He loved our mother because she had blessed him with two sons and for a ruler like him, there was nothing better than having two male heirs. Then he met Zara's mother, daughter of an English nobleman, in London and he brought her here, announcing that he would get married to her."

Nasrin took a small sip of her wine, listening to me.

"She was kind and sweet. Treated us like her own. Until she got pregnant and gave birth to my half-sister, Zara," I smiled, remembering the day. "We all adored Zara. Her pale cheeks were like two big cherries when she was a baby. Khalid wouldn't stop crying when he took her in his arms for the first time, even though she pooped on him."

We both shared a small laugh before I continued. "Unfortunately, my father didn't want a female heir from our new mother. He changed. He would berate and chastise us. Then one night, we heard the screams of our mother, our father… punishing her for not giving him another boy."

I clenched my hands into fists and looked away. "Khalid and I tried to stop him, and he hit both of us. It hurt him, but he didn't cry. He suffered through it. It stopped after that for a while, but we knew we could not trust our father with our sister."

"Our mothers passed away when they were flying to London for a few weeks. The airplane had crashed and both of them died instantly. Our father didn't take it very well. He would get drunk and have lavish parties and parade his sons, Khalid and I, to his guests, daring others to ever stand against Azmia. While he forced Zara to her room, never to be seen by anyone. He hated her. It was terrible. I thought the alcohol and parties helped him. That our father had gotten better, but we were fools."

Her hand landed on my closed fists, "Zain… you—"

I pinned my gaze on her. "You need to know the truth,

Nasrin. You need to know what a terrible person Salman Al Latif was and why we hate him."

Taking a deep breath, I continued, "Zara had turned six. He would never allow Zara outside of the palace, and even to certain rooms, because he was ashamed of having a female child. His thinking was old-fashioned, he only thought of her as an object to trade for better alliance. Khalid and I tried our best to make her happy and protect her from him. But we barely could. He asked her to his room one night and when Khalid got there, he saw Zara crying and begging Khalid to take her away from there. Our father wanted her to accept a marriage proposal from a sheikh."

"She was six, for fuck's sake! He dared to force her to accept a betrothal when she was supposed to play with other kids and grow, not think about marriage. When I reached the room, I tried to talk with him, but he hit me and in anger, he was ready to hit our sister, but Khalid protected her like he always did."

"What happened, Zain? Was Khalid harmed?"

"Khalid killed him." I swallowed the lump in my throat, looking away from her. "He used our father's own sword and plunged it through his chest before he could harm anyone else. Zara was hugging Khalid and crying for him while I told the guards to not enter the room."

"I had to do something. I couldn't protect my mothers, my sister and my brother, so I made sure that the murder of my father would never be known."

I thought about that night, the shocked faces of my brother and sister, utterly confused and scared and looking at me for help.

"The advisor, Rahim, guided me with everything. He was the one who announced that my father passed away in his sleep and I would be crowned as the sultan. He was relieved that Azmia would have a better sultan ruling over it, and our family was safe from any harm. When I became the sultan, I vowed to never turn myself into the monster my father was."

"You are not like him, Zain," Nasrin whispered, cupping my jaw to make me look at her. Tears glistened in her brown umber eyes.

"But the apple doesn't fall far from the tree, does it?"

Her eyes swirled, and she leaned closer. "You are not your father, Zain. He chose to harm others, and you vowed to protect them. Zara and Khalid, and even the people of Azmia, look up to you. They feel safe because they know that Sultan Zain will protect them no matter what." Her voice was firm, her hand lowering to my chest, pressing against my heart. "And above all, you have a kind heart, Zain."

I didn't know why tears stung in my eyes, burning them. I held her palm that was on my chest and kissed the soft skin. "Thank you, Nasrin."

"May I kiss you, Sultan?"

My eyes flitted to her face, her lips, her warm eyes. I swallowed, my voice thick when I said, "Kiss me all you want, Sultana. I am yours."

Her lips met mine in a gentle caress, barely touching, teasing me. With a low growl, I pulled her closer, her legs straddling my hips. Our bodies pressed against each other, my hands exploring the curves and dips of her body. I listened to the little sighs and gasps she made when I glided my hands over the round of her ass, the softness of her breasts over her dress.

"I need more, Zain," she whispered, pulling away. Her lips were wet and swollen with the kisses, her eyes dark underneath the moonlight. "I need you."

I caressed her cheek. "Are you sure?"

"Yes, are you, Sultan?"

"I want to have you under me, above me and in every way possible, Nasrin," I said, my voice low and husky.

She shivered and didn't waste any time kissing me. I gently tugged at her hair, setting it loose and raking my hand through it when our kiss turned passionate. I could feel my muscles clench and relax when she touched me, removing the suit jacket and unbuttoning the buttons of my shirt.

"Then have me anywhere you want," Nasrin said, her voice sultry, kissing my neck, my Adam's apple, my chest.

Her nails scratched over my abs, making me groan when her breasts brushed over the bulge in my pants. Nasrin's eyes turned darker, hooded with lust, when they flickered from my face to my pants. I bit my lip and watched my beautiful wife undo my belt.

"May I?"

"Yes," I replied, my voice lowering an octave. "I want to see you naked first."

"Yes, Your Majesty," Nasrin teased, leaning up on her knees and removing the straps of her dress. I helped her remove the dress and swore under my breath. She wasn't wearing a bra that whole time. Her breasts were round, with dusky nipples poking through the cool air. I swallowed the lump in my throat, noticing the black lace thong covering her heated sex.

"You are beautiful, Nasrin," I whispered, cupping her cheek and gently kissing her lips. She let out a soft moan, her fingers threading my hair. I pulled away and rubbed the pad of my thumb over her bottom full lip. "I have a wish."

"What is it?" she asked, her voice breathy.

"I want you to show me how you pleasure yourself. Show me how you touch your pussy."

Her cheeks turned red, the candles and lantern around the balcony casting a soft glow on us. "But you—"

"What? You will deny your sultan's one wish?" I mocked. "*Show me* how you touch yourself."

"Zain…" she whispered, her lips parted.

"Yes?" I asked, raising my brow, trailing my hand over her sides and softly kneading her heavy breasts. She whimpered above me when I tweaked and rolled her nipples with my fingers.

"I… I will do it," she said. "But you have to do it with me too."

I frowned. "Have you never seen a male touch himself before?"

Nasrin laughed and *fuck me*, I wanted to make her laugh again, hear it over and over again. "It doesn't matter, I want to see you when I pleasure myself."

I watched her splay herself across the low table that was draped with dark red velvet. She sat on the table, her stunning body perched directly across from me, my eyes trailing over every inch of her. A cool breeze ruffled the strands of her hair. I licked my lips and leaned back a little when she pulled down her underwear with a shy smile playing across her lips.

Then she spread her legs. Wide.

Clenching my jaw, I tried to control myself from wanting to taste the glistening wetness of her pussy. The scent of her feminine arousal coated the air. The sound of water in the pool splashing surrounded us.

"Touch yourself, Nasrin," I said. "Let your Sultan watch."

23

NASRIN

The way he said it and ordered my body to move on his command was surreal. His onyx eyes were pinned on me, raking over my body as if he was touching me and licking every inch of my skin. I watched him lean back, his powerful, muscular body glowing in the moonlight. Every contour of his abs and muscles of his golden skin were on display.

Keeping my mouth from watering, I leaned back, my ass perched on the velvet fabric, and lowered my hand from my aching breasts to my waist. His eyes followed my hands, his own fingers working on the zipper of his pants. Lower. I sighed, closing my eyes when my fingers caressed the sensitive clit.

"Open your eyes and look at me, Nasrin," he said, his voice laced with arousal.

I did, and watched him through my lashes. My powerful sultan. My handsome husband. My Zain.

My eyes trailed over his body, his hands lowering the dark boxers. I licked my lips at the sight of his cock, the tip leaking with precum, when he gently stroked his veiny shaft.

I watched him and he watched me. My fingers slick with juices as I pushed them inside me, rubbing my clit with the other hand.

"Zain…" I moaned.

"Nasrin," he groaned. The sounds of our pleasures surrounded us. Our eyes flickered over each other's naked bodies, wanting to watch each other come apart with pleasure.

I held onto his shoulder when I rubbed my fingers over the sensitive spot inside me and increasing the pressure on the swollen nub. Zain caressed my waist, his large hand pumping himself, the erotic sounds of his groans sending shivers down my spine, making me cream more.

I climaxed first, my legs trembling with the overpowering orgasm rocking through my body. Squeezing my eyes shut, I let myself sink into the white fiery lust, my body burning. His hand held onto me, gliding over my soft skin, saying my name, whispering it against my neck and groaning against my ear when he reached his own peak.

Zain shuddered, his warm breath fanning over my skin as I watched him reach his peak with half-lidded eyes. His dark golden skin trembling when he came in his hand, his seed coating the insides of my thigh.

"*Fuck*," he breathed, his dark eyes hazy with pleasure when he watched me through his thick lashes. "That was the hardest I have ever come, Nasrin. I want to see you climax again."

"Again?"

"I can never tire from the sight of my beautiful wife moaning my name and reaching her orgasm."

I blushed at his words. "You are a dirty, wild sultan, Zain."

He gave me a small smile and apologized to me, cleaning my inner thigh with his expensive shirt. Before he could clean himself, I lowered myself from the low table and kneeled across him on the soft fabric of the seating.

"Allow me, Sultan," I said, waiting for him to consent.

He clenched his jaw, his eyes gleaming when they trailed over my naked body. He nodded, pulling me close and kissing me on the lips before allowing me to do whatever I wanted with him.

I pressed sweet kisses over his chest, his abs, and watched them tense and relax under my touch. Kissing down the sharp vee of his hip bones, I lowered myself until I was face to face with his semi-hard length.

Flickering my eyes to his face, I stroked him slowly, squeezing his girthy shaft. I leaned down and licked the tip, humming at his musky male scent. I loved the way he tasted. Dipping lower, I took him in my mouth, hollowing my cheeks as I sucked him while stroking the base with my hand.

"Nasrin," Zain groaned, his hand threading in my hair.

I pulled away to lick his length, the veins, and swirl my tongue around the head of his cock. He groaned again when I took him in my warm mouth, my hands holding onto his powerful thighs. Relaxing my throat, I took him deeper, but before I could properly deep throat him, he pulled me away.

He was panting hard, his erect length jutting out to his stomach when he gazed at me. I licked my lips, wondering if I didn't do a good job. "What happened? Did I do something wrong?" I asked.

Zain shook his head and laid me down on the soft velvet of the seating. "I didn't want to release inside your mouth," he whispered, hovering above me and kissing me gently.

"But I wanted you to," I confessed.

"Maybe some other time," he said, leaning back on his knees, staring at my naked body sprawled across him. "I need to have you, Nasrin. Make sweet love to you."

My eyes burned when I gazed at him. *This beautiful, sweet man wanted to make love to me.* Nodding at him, I spread my legs wider. "Make love to me, Zain."

His warm hands gliding over my thighs, his eyes eyeing my heated sex. "*Oh...*" I moaned when he leaned down and pressed his mouth against my pussy.

Zain groaned, his lips licking and sucking over my sensitive clit. My back arched off the soft fabric when he placed my legs over his shoulders, spreading my legs wider. My fingers tugged at his thick dark hair, my long moans encouraging him when he dipped his finger inside me. I wanted to squeeze my eyes shut and enjoy the immense pleasure he was giving me, but all I could focus on was his onyx eyes. They gazed at me while he languorously ate me out.

"Zain," I breathed out. "Please, I can't hold back any longer."

He pulled away, licking his lips and humming as if he was having a delicious treat. My mouth went dry when I watched him pull out his finger, glistening with my arousal, and place it on my bottom lip.

"Taste how sweet you are, Nasrin," he whispered, urging me to wrap my lips around his finger, licking the sweet, musky taste of myself.

His eyes were dark, like two obsidian pools when he settled himself over me, the large expanse of his muscular body hovering above me. I spread my legs to accommodate him, taking a sharp breath when I felt him brush through my entrance.

"Is it okay?" I asked him, cupping his jaw.

Zain smiled at me, kissing the corner of my lips. "Yes, my wife. Tell me if I am doing anything wrong, okay? I don't want to cause you any pain."

"You won't, Zain." My fingers feathered over the nape of

his neck as I wrapped my legs around his hips, "Please don't make me wait."

Taking a deep breath, he pressed his stiffened length against my dripping sex. I curled my fingers around his shoulder when he slid inside, his girthy shaft stretching my walls. I gasped. He groaned. My entire body was burning when he filled me up, inch by inch, to the hilt.

Zain swore under his breath, his fingers clenching the fabric underneath me. I urged him closer, my walls clenching him with need. "I need you to move, Zain. *Please.*"

Kissing my neck, he looked down at our adjoined bodies, groaning at the view as he reared back and slowly slid inside me. He held me with care, his hand holding my hip, when he pulled back and slowly increased his pace. Our moans surrounded us, the air coated with the scent of our arousal, the sound of skin slapping against each other.

Zain made love to me under the night sky full of stars.

It was sweet, hot, and sweaty.

I held onto his shoulders, encouraging my husband, my sultan, to go faster and deeper until we reached our own high, moaning against each other's skin when we came apart.

We embraced each other when the aftershocks of our orgasms rocked through our body. I trailed my hand over his body, over his face, kissing him when his glazed eyes met mine.

"Come here," he whispered, kissing my hair and wrapping his arms around me, snuggling me.

I smiled, kissing his chest and hearing the steady sound of his heart. My eyes on the twinkling stars before sleep overtook me.

"Fuck," I breathed, threading my fingers through his hair when he plunged inside me.

Zain's jaw was clenched, holding my waist as the edge of the desk dug into my ass while he fucked me in his study. It had been a few weeks since our date night on the roof where we had sex for the first time after getting married. Since then, it was like a switch had been flicked on that changed both of our libidos for the better, and we both couldn't get enough of each other.

Always sneaking away or meeting somewhere in the palace because of our busy schedules and losing ourselves in each other's bodies. I was always on my toes wondering how he would use his tongue, which position he would fuck me, and how he would order me to stay quiet, to not get caught. It was thrilling.

I moaned, trying to stifle it into his shirt, which smelt heavenly from his musky cologne. "Harder, Zain. I am so close," I whimpered, lowering my hand to hold on to his arms, the sleeves of his shirt rolled over his elbows.

"Hang in there, Nasrin," he whispered, looking down between us, watching our unison and using his thumb to rub my sensitive nub.

We both released together after two more thrusts, my toes curling in my sandals and body writhing as he held me close when our orgasms rocked through both of us.

"Are you okay?" he asked, his voice deep and husky when he pulled away, fixing his clothes.

"I am."

"That's good—*shit*. I didn't use a condom," Zain swore, quickly cleaning himself with tissues and apologizing to me constantly and dialing a number on his phone. "It's okay, I will talk to a doctor and we can have a checkup just to make sure we are not..."

He cut his words off when the doctor picked up the

phone. I had already straightened out my dress and seeing my husband panic so much because he was afraid of forgetting to use a condom once irked me. I had noticed, however horny we might be, he always made sure he was wearing protection.

That might be the first time I had felt him raw inside me since we'd married.

I leaned on my toes and ended the call before he could book our appointment with the doctor. I ignored his shocked look and said, "You don't have to worry so much for not wearing a condom once, Zain. I am on birth control pills. I have told you before."

"But you know I liked having an extra layer of protection in case… in case something happens."

I deadpanned, "In case I get pregnant?"

Zain sighed, running a hand through his hair. "I don't want to talk to you about it right now, Nasrin."

I watched him finish buttoning his shirt and organize the papers on his desk that we had ruffled. Taking a deep breath, I asked, "Would it be so bad to have a child with me, Zain?"

He replied without a pause, "Yes."

I could see the widening of his eyes at the truth he had just blurted. I straightened my spine and held my chin high as I turned and walked out of the study before he could see the gleam of tears in my eyes. I should have known better. At the end of the day, I was his wife and Sultana of Azmia, just as a title. He didn't see me as his wife. I was foolish to think that something might have changed between us after all this time.

2 4

ZAIN

I had lunch in my study, trying my best to ignore the lingering scent of jasmine and musky feminine scent. I had told her that having a child, getting her pregnant, was a terrible idea. I was stupid.

Groaning, I pinched the bridge of my nose. I didn't mean to voice it like that, but I was annoyed with myself for forgetting to wear protection when I knew the risks. The risk of having a baby and turning into my father. Hurting both Nasrin and our child. I couldn't bear to think about it.

"You called me, Sultan?" One of the staff entered the study, bowing his head.

"Arrange a different room for me tonight," I said and added, "Don't let Sultana worry about it."

He frowned, wanting to question me, but he knew who I was. So he agreed and left, leaving me to reflect on my choices.

After seeing her hurt and angry with me, I knew spending the night together in one room was the last thing she wanted. I didn't want to cause her any more trouble than I already had.

"WHY DIDN'T YOU HAVE DINNER WITH US?" ZARA ASKED, walking with me and Khalid in the gardens. We used to do that a lot when we were kids, telling her about flowers and playing with her.

Khalid gave me a look and said, "Because he and Nasrin had their first fight."

I scowled at him and crossed my arms. The wind was cold, and it reminded me of the night where I had walked the same cobblestone path with her. I wished she had joined us, but Khalid told me she left for her room as soon as she had dinner.

"Really?" Zara frowned. "I hope you apologize to her."

"Why do you think it's my fault?"

Khalid snickered and my sister raised her brow at me. "Isn't it? You always skipped having to eat with us whenever you thought you were guilty. You couldn't bear to be in the same room, let alone eat. So your absence from dinner meant it was your fault and—"

"Yes, Zara, you're right." I looked away, embarrassed.

"What happened?" Khalid asked after a few moments.

I swallowed the lump in my throat. "I was brutally honest with her and my answer hurt her. I want to talk with her, but I am afraid."

Zara giggled. "Stop being a pussy and just talk to her, geez."

Khalid and I groaned hearing our little sister curse.

"What?" Zara said.

"Take some time tonight and talk to her first thing in the morning. Be honest, don't sugarcoat things," my brother advised, and I took mental notes. Even though he had never been in a relationship, he was wise. He had been infatuated with only one girl since I can remember, but he doesn't share anything about her because he thinks that he would never find her.

"And don't go empty-handed. Women love gifts, especially from the people we love," Zara cooed, giving me ideas of what to gift her. Chocolates, a movie date night, books or even perfume. Azmia was well-known for the rich scent of our exotic perfumes, and before I met Nasrin, I had asked to have a custom-made perfume with a note of jasmine. I could gift it to her.

"I will talk to her," I announced and forced them into a hug, ignoring Khalid's whine. "Thank you."

♛

"What did you want to talk about, Sultan?" Nasrin asked, her voice monotone as she looked anywhere but at me.

I had missed her. Sleeping in another room without the bedsheets and pillows smelling like her or the press of her warm body against mine had made me sleepless. I had resisted the urge of waking her up at midnight to apologize and sleep with her.

"I wanted to apologize to you. I am sorry, Nasrin. I didn't mean to sound so harsh when I answered your question," I said to her, wishing I could step closer to her and embrace her.

She bit her lip and looked away, a lock of dark hair brushing her collarbone. "As much as your answer hurt me, Zain, you shouldn't apologize to me. I am sorry for even thinking that you would want to have a child. Especially with me. You had made it clear that you didn't—"

"Nasrin. Do you know why I don't want children? Because I hate the thought of having our child, loving him or her. It pains me to think that I will turn out worse than my father was and hurt you and our child. I have nightmares about it because following my father's footsteps is the last thing that I want."

I closed my eyes because I couldn't look at her after telling her the truth. She had asked me to always be honest with her before we got married. It felt good to be honest about it, but I was afraid of what she might think of me for having such terrible thoughts.

"Zain." I shuddered when her fingers cupped my cheeks. I opened my eyes and stared at her, her eyes gleaming as tears slid down her face. "You are not him. You are Zain. You are my Zain, and you don't need to prove to yourself or anyone that you are not like your father. Everyone knows that you are not. We don't need to have a child if that's what you want. I am sorry for being so annoying yesterday and a—"

"Please don't cry," I whispered, wiping away her tears and embracing her in a hug. "I will try not to compare myself with him, but it will take time, Nasrin. But I will try because I don't want you to be angry at me. I want to be better for you."

"You are better for me, Zain."

I pulled away and cupped her cheeks, gazing at her glittering brown eyes. "I won't deny that I am terrified, but I am more thrilled to have a baby with you, Nasrin. I know you would smack me before I do something stupid, so all I want to do is ask a favor from you."

"What?" Her voice was barely audible.

"Be with me. Stay with me when I make stupid decisions and scold me."

"Are you sure? That sounds really good to me. I love scolding the most powerful sultan."

I let out a soft laugh, her grin making my heartbeat increase. "Yes, I am sure, Sultana. You look hot when you are angry."

Nasrin scrunched her face and let out a loud laugh that made me feel something weird in my stomach. My eyes noticed and captured every little detail of her. The sound of her laugh doing odd things to my body.

Is this what it was? Is this how it feels to be in love?

I held her hand, my thumb brushing over her knuckles. "Nasrin, I lo—"

"Sultan!"

I closed my eyes and sighed at the knock on our door. My guards had terrible timing.

"Can we continue our talk later?" she asked with a small grin.

"Yes, we will. I need to tell the guards not to knock whenever I am with you."

"That's stupid. What if it's an emergency?"

"You make me feel like doing stupid things."

I laughed when she pinched my arm.

♛

"And then the Sheikh was upset hearing that Nasrin has already been wed to you. I'd never dream of my daughter marrying that old man anyway, but a father's main duty is to make sure his daughter weds and is in a suitable home. You know what I mean, Sultan. Pass me some more wine, will you?" Nasrin's father, Hamid Elbaz, laughed yet again, ignoring the odd looks of everyone, and took the whole tumbler of wine and filled his cup once again.

The guards had announced that Nasrin's father had come here to visit, and before we had lunch together, I had given them privacy to talk. Looking at the small frown on my wife's face, I knew something had happened.

"I disagree," Zara said, staring directly at him. Nasrin clenched her hand around me, and I squeezed it back in reassurance. My sister could handle herself. It was her father that I was afraid for.

"Excuse me, child?"

Khalid clenched his jaw, glaring at him, but held back from retorting.

"It's Princess Zara. I hope you don't forget that in the future." My sister gave him a sweet smile. "And I completely disagree with your opinion. I believe that parents' primary concern should be to provide for their children, educate them, and make sure their kids can live on their own when they grow up."

Nasrin's father looked troubled. His face had turned red while everyone nodded hearing my sister's words. "But you are a child, Princess. You wouldn't know what it is like to be a father."

"I am nineteen and old enough to know that if you had taught your sons some polite manners, they wouldn't mock other women in their court. Didn't your eldest son assault a young man even though he is a sultan?" Zara tsked, shaking her head. "I would certainly be ashamed of myself if I were you and teach him a lesson rather than shaming my daughter for not being pregnant so soon after her marriage."

My head snapped at Nasrin, her head dipping. "Did he shame you for that?" I whispered and glared at her father when she nodded.

Nasrin pretended to drink wine. Khalid looked proud and my grandmother nodded before resuming their lunch. Only Nasrin's father looked furious, glaring at my sister when she took a sip of wine from her glass.

"Forgive me, son-in-law, but you need to teach some manners to your sister on how to address her elders and give them respect. If I were you, I would make sure that she apologized and ate nothing until she le—"

"I am not sure your tongue is precious to you, Hamid

Elbaz," Khalid said in a silent voice. "Because if it was, you would want it attached to that filthy face of yours before you leave Azmia."

Everyone held their breath after hearing my brother's not-so-silent threat. Zara cleared her throat and resumed her lunch. So did Khalid. The tension was heavy and thick in the hall, but we all knew who was in the right and who was in the wrong.

The way her father acted disgusted me. I wondered how Nasrin spent so many years growing up under the same roof as that man.

"You heard the Prince, *baba*. Do not mock my sister or attempt to threaten her again," Nasrin spoke up, her voice stern. "Or as the Sultana of Azmia, I will make sure you do not step in my country ever again."

I squeezed her hand for standing up to her father. If we had been alone, I would have kissed her and I have to remember to do it as soon as we get alone. Maybe we could spend some time alone in the afternoon, because seeing her give out a command as sultana and politely threaten her father was the hottest thing I had seen. It aroused me to see her like that.

"S-sultan?" Her father stammered when he looked at me, utterly in disbelief at the way his own daughter had reacted.

"You heard the order of Sultana." I lazily took a sip of the bitter red wine. "I am afraid you need to learn some manners if you want to visit Azmia again."

He gaped at me, at all of us, even my grandma who was busy scolding the staff to bring her another glass of wine, saying things were getting interesting. He pushed the plate and stood up, anger written all over his face as he trembled.

"I didn't ask you to leave yet. Please be polite and sit down," I said, ordering him to sit. Even the guards behind him stepped forward.

"This lunch is nothing but a mocking—"

I interrupted him, "Apologize to your daughter for what you said to her this morning."

His nose flared, glaring at his own daughter. Khalid was tense, holding the fork in his hand tightly. I just prayed that Hamid wouldn't spew any more stupidity or else Khalid would fulfill his threat to him. With a fork, if it came to be.

"Apologize. Now."

He looked at her, Nasrin's face devoid of any emotion, when her father said, "I apologize for my behavior, Nasrin."

"You are forgiven," she replied.

"You may leave." I waved my hand, and the guards moved away. "But remember that I do not take threats to my family lightly. I hope you remember that on your next visit to Azmia. I hope your stay was well."

Rahim stopped him, his eyes fixing on me as he bowed. "I am afraid, Sultan and Sultana, that Hamid Elbaz can't leave just yet."

"What do you mean?" he bellowed, his face red with anger.

"What is it, Rahim? Did something happen?" I asked, not enjoying the tension hovering in the air. Everyone looked uncomfortable.

"There is something you need to hear, Sultan," he said. "Alone."

Nasrin's hand clenched around me, her expression worried.

"It's okay, you can share it with me and my family," I announced, all the other guests leaving their seats. I, along with Nasrin and my siblings remained seated. I didn't want to trouble Grandmother, so I asked her maids to walk her to her room. Nasrin's father glared at all of us as he was forced to sit down on the chair.

"If that's what you wish," Rahim said, and fixed his eyes

on Hamid. "Do you want to tell us what happened when their mothers left for London?"

My spine straightened, so did Khalid's. "What is this about?"

Hamid's face drained of color and he looked at us, his daughter, before averting his eyes. "I don't know what you are talking about."

"Rahim, what is this about?" I repeated once again, my voice hard.

My advisor looked at me, his eyes softening. "I am sorry to be a bearer of this news, Sultan… and Sultana. But Hamid Elbaz planned the death of your mothers. That airplane crash was intentional. He wanted to kill them so he could weaken Salman Al Latif and fight Azmia from him."

My heart dropped in my stomach, my ears ringing. I shook my head, "That couldn't be… why would he kill them to fight Azmia?"

"Is this true, *baba*?" Nasrin's voice was weak when she looked across the table.

Her father did not meet her eyes.

"Did you kill my mothers?" Khalid asked, standing up from the chair. I could see what was running through his eyes. The anger and the silent threat in his voice.

I stopped him, holding him back before he could kill Hamid Elbaz. "Hear him out, Khalid."

"He killed our mothers. I don't want to hear from him. I want to ki—"

"*Khalid*," Zara said, her face ashen as she looked at us. They were her mothers, too. "Please, let us hear what he has to say."

Once we were all settled down, one of the guards stepped forward with a small knife pointed to Hamid's neck. I didn't look at Nasrin.

"Speak," I ordered.

He swallowed the lump in his throat, his withered face scrunching. "It wasn't supposed to end up like that. I had envied Salman since the day both of us were crowned as sultans. He was my friend, but I envied him. His riches, his charm, his strength. That envy and greed for more made me want to take Azmia from him. The only thing, his country, that he ever cared about. He didn't even care about his wives or his children. I had seen him laugh about them, mock them, I couldn't understand how a powerful man like him could be so cruel towards his own family."

My jaw clenched when he continued, his eyes looking at me. "So, I planned to kill him. To do that, I became his close friend and learned that he would visit London, leaving his wives and children in the palace. I had a bomb planted in his private plane but I didn't know that he would change his plans last minute. That he stayed back in the palace and let his wives go to London."

I closed my eyes and took a shaky breath. He had planted a bomb on the plane that killed my mothers. He was the reason that our father mourned for them and hurt us more.

"Sultan, we have to—"

I stopped Rahim from speaking and stood up. Khalid and Zara didn't look too well. I glared at the man for the root cause of our pain. "Take him to the dungeons. He isn't allowed to leave Azmia until he is ready to announce his crimes publicly."

I left when the guards took him away, ignoring his pleading when he begged his own daughter to help him. I could hear Nasrin following me, calling me to stop and talk to her.

"I can't talk to you. You are the daughter of the person who killed my mothers," I said, hating the tone of my voice.

"Don't tell me you believe that I had something to do with it," she whispered harshly, holding my wrist and making me face her. "I am sorry for what my father did, but you have to trust me I had nothing to do with it, Zain. I... I like you, I have feelings for you, and if I had known the truth, which I didn't, I would have told you."

"Or you married me because you knew I wasn't like my father. That I would share equal power and responsibilities with you so you could scheme whatever you wanted with your family to take Azmia from me."

She took a step back, her hand pressing against her mouth. "You don't mean any of that..."

I gritted my teeth. "I don't and that's the problem, because that's what the council and the people of our countries will think when the news of your father's deeds come out. There will be a council meeting, and they will give your father the death penalty if he accepts his crimes, Nasrin."

Her eyes watered and I hated that I couldn't step towards her and tell her everything would be okay and I would keep her safe. Instead, I continued, thinking like a sultan rather than the Zain she adored. "They will question your entire family. Even you."

"I don't care," she cried out. "I want to hear what you will do, Zain. Please tell me you—"

"You should go back," I said in a bitter voice. "Go to Maahnoor. Your presence here might affect the judgement of your father and your family's questioning."

"Zain, don't make me go away. I am a sultana, I can help you and we can sort it—"

My heart broke when I said, "I am ordering you as the Sultan to leave Azmia and visit your home. You must miss Maahnoor. Don't come back until they announce you not guilty, Nasrin."

I hated myself when I walked away from her, ignoring the instinct to go back and tell her it would be okay. That I wouldn't let anyone harm her, and I would keep her safe and make sure no harm came to her family.

But I couldn't do that. Because even as the most powerful sultan in the Middle East, I couldn't protect her. Those words were nothing but a lie, and I couldn't lie to the person I loved.

25

NASRIN

"You have to eat something."

As if prodded by my younger brother's command, my stomach growled. "See? Starving yourself won't bring you any joy, Nasrin. Eat," Imran said, taking a piece of my favorite sweet *kunafah*, and twirling it across my face.

"Stop it," I grumbled and shuffled on the bed. The same old white-washed, simple bed in the Maahnoor palace. "I don't want to eat anything right now."

Imran sighed. His warm brown eyes had lost the gleam they had since the news of my father's crime. "You have been saying that for the past three days. Look at yourself in the mirror, you look worse than Sadiq did when he woke up after Hussain pranked him with the laxatives in his food for his thirtieth birthday."

I cracked a small smile, remembering that day. Hussain was a year older than me and younger than Sadiq. Both of us were middle children, and we loved to spend time together.

"Where is he? He would be questioned too."

Imran shrugged. "Last we heard, he was in one of our

oases doing God knows what. The council hasn't started interviewing us so that's good."

It wasn't good. He was being optimistic. The council consisted of all the sultans and their advisors, to keep all the countries in unity and look out for each other. If Zain wanted to execute our entire family for our father's crime, he could.

"Are the guards bothering you?" I asked.

"They are not. We can live with that for a few days. I am worried about Sadiq. He hasn't left his room since the news… he won't open the door to his room and there are more guards around him."

Being the Sultan of Maahnoor, he would be guarded well. Since the day I had arrived in Maahnoor, the palace loitered with men and women in dark suits that hid their weapons, even though they treated us as royalty. I didn't know whether they were here for our protection or something else. It bothered me.

How my life had changed in a day. From the Sultana of Azmia to a caged royal prisoner. I wished I could see Zain's handsome face again so I could punch him. He was a jerk to cage me inside my own palace, and I wouldn't ever forgive him for that. No matter how much I loved him.

"You should leave. They will get suspicious," I said to Imran. Before he could say anything, I added, "Yes, I will eat everything. Thank you."

"Don't thank me, Nasrin. As your brother, it is my duty to keep my sister safe and healthy." He kissed my forehead and left the room, the female guards doing their regular checks to see if my brother had handed me any weapon or not.

I let them. It was their duty to check and report back to the council, and especially my husband, who had banished me from Azmia.

"Everything's clear, you can have your lunch, Sultana," the

woman with blonde hair smiled at me with a bow, her holsters fitted with two guns as she unbuttoned her suit. I had noticed her mostly around the palace, but for the last two days, she had been around my room a lot.

"You don't have to call me that. I am not a sultana anymore," I answered, feeling a little intimidated by her intelligent, green eyes. She seemed too pretty with the guns, and I didn't want to tick her off by saying anything wrong. Even though her warm smile felt friendly.

"Bullshit, you are a sultana. That too of Azmia," she said. "Trust me, Zain isn't stupid, and he will take you out of here before you know it. Think of it as a mini vacation."

"How do you know Zain?" *And how dare you call him by his first name.*

"It's a long story—oh, is that *kunafah*. I love *kunafah*! Do you mind if I take a small bite? Please? I will bring you anyone's head you want!" She cooed, her eyes pleading.

I blinked at her. "Head?"

She nodded. "Yes, your enemy or someone you hate."

My eyes widened, and I gave her a once over. *Who is she?* I cleared my throat and shook my head. "No, that's alright. I don't want anyone's head. You can take a bite."

"Thank you!" She practically bounced towards the sweet and took the small bite which my brother had torn for me. Before she put it in her mouth, she sniffed it and took a step back.

Her green eyes widened when she looked at me, "Please tell me you didn't eat anything from that plate."

I shook my head, confused by her actions. "I didn't."

She nodded at me, "Good." Taking the plate, she opened the door to my room and handed it to another guard, whispering something in his ear.

"What happened? That was my lunch." My stomach growled with sadness.

"I am sorry, Sultana. Your lunch will be with you in a few minutes with a royal tester in tow."

"I don't need a royal tester," I laughed, thinking about someone tasting my food before me.

"Yes, you do. That *kunafah* was poisoned." Her tone was firm.

"Who would do that to me?" I almost squeaked, clutching my stomach.

"You are a ruler of Azmia whose father committed a heinous crime. Of course, some people would want you either dead or as a hostage," she said casually, as if she was talking to me about her favorite colors.

"Don't worry, I will make sure no harm comes your way, Your Grace. Please eat the food only after the tester has eaten a bite of everything."

I nodded, still confused, when the door of my room was closed. I sat on the edge of the bed, wondering what had happened.

♛

IMRAN HAD BEEN FURIOUS WHEN HE GOT THE NEWS OF MY food poisoning. He had apologized to me when the cook who had emptied the poison in my food had been caught in less than a day. He considered himself guilty for trying to make me eat my favorite sweet. But it wasn't his fault. The same cook had poisoned his and Sadiq's lunch.

The blonde guard had told me that the cook would be sent to Azmia and questioned there by the Sultan himself and then executed.

I didn't like whatever was happening around me. As soon as I was ready to accept my feelings towards Zain, he forced me to leave Azmia instead of trying to hear me out. My family and I were being kept like caged birds in the walls of the palace, always surrounded by the guards with a threat to our lives.

Why did he have to make me leave? I hate him.

26
ZAIN

"What other crimes have you committed?" I asked, the dim light of the prison casting a yellow shadow on Hamid Elbaz's bruised face. The stench of sweat, blood and something rancid coated the air, making it hard to breathe. These dungeons, under the palace of Azmia, were used by our ancestors during the wars to keep the prisoners, and we had kept them just in case we had to use them again.

Khalid didn't want him to sit or sleep, but I had been merciful to allow him a chair and sleep and food.

"I already told you," he rasped, his voice scratchy. He tried to move, but his hands were tied behind the chair and his ankles to the legs of the chair.

The interviewer shuffled forward, scared of me and my brother more than the person who sat in the chair. "Right." The man cleared his throat and fixed his tie. "Can I start now?"

"He is all yours," Khalid drawled, sliding his hands in his pockets and watching the interview take place.

It had been four days, six hours and forty minutes since

I last saw Nasrin. I missed her terribly, hating that I couldn't protect her when someone tried to poison her food. I should have known that something might have happened, and I should have acted on it. Instead, I was busy with the council meetings, agreeing to get Hamid Elbaz executed and making sure they found his children not guilty. Hamid had said so himself that they had nothing to do with his crimes, especially Nasrin. She was a kid when that had happened and she was the most innocent of all his four children.

I believed him. Nasrin knew nothing about her father's past. She had cried listening to him confess about it that day. She didn't think her father could ever do that. That was why I needed to push her away and to show the council that my decision to have Hamid Elbaz executed and protect her family had nothing to do with my marital relationship with her. If she had stayed here, they would have questioned her about terrible things, and I wouldn't have been able to protect her from it.

After getting Hamid's confession on tape, the interviewer from the famous news channel stepped out with his camera crew, leaving me, Khalid and the prisoner.

"Don't hurt my Nasrin," he said in a hoarse voice. "Please, I beg you."

My brother clenched his jaw. I glared down at his face. "She is not yours anymore, Hamid. She is the Sultana of Azmia and my wife."

He chuckled weakly. "I am glad she has you. She deserves the love you have for her. I couldn't ever provide her with everything she wanted, but you can." His head dropped and I forced myself to take a step back when his eyes teared up. "Tell my children I am sorry, even though it means nothing. I am ready to be punished for my sins."

We left, the sight of him breaking down ingrained in my

head. The guard asked us about the other prisoner. The cook who had poisoned my wife's and her brothers' food.

I didn't give it a second thought before replying, "Get his confession and kill him."

Khalid stopped me. "Keep him alive, Zain."

"Why?" I flared my nose. "He dared to go against Azmia and poison the Sultana. My wife. He doesn't deserve to live."

"True, but keep him alive down here. He will be useful to us," my brother said, looking at me.

I trusted Khalid. If he wanted to keep him alive, then I would do it. I nodded to the guard. "You heard the Prince. But don't tell anyone about his whereabouts or that he is alive. Keep him fed and breathing."

♛

"You look pathetic," my grandmother greeted us when we joined her for dinner. Even Zara was silent when the food was served.

"That is the face of the stubborn man who misses his wife terribly," Zayed said, pouring a glass of wine for me which I swallowed in one gulp. Khalid eyed me warily.

"I miss her, but I can't go against the council and bring her back here until they execute her father," I said, frowning at the food. I didn't feel like eating but forced it down because I would need the strength.

"Do you truly want her back?" Grandmother asked after a while.

I didn't even hesitate. "Yes."

"Then go and get her. You are the Sultan of Azmia who misses his wife. Even your own people want their sultana back in their country. I am sure the council can overlook it."

No one said anything, but my grandmother's message was clear. *Go and get Nasrin, or I will be disappointed in you.*

Should I try to get her back? It wasn't like I could knock on the palace gates and they would happily let me in. She might hate me for what I had done, curse at me, and even throw her sandals at me. But I could handle all of that if it meant seeing her and knowing she was well. I would try to woo her, apologize to her, and do my best to get her back.

Because everybody was right. I missed her. Her absence spoke volumes whenever she wasn't teasing me in the study, taking care of our horses in the stables, laughing with Zara and my family, mocking me in our bathroom suite just because I liked to wet my toothbrush after applying toothpaste. I missed her every day I woke up alone in our bed and went to sleep on the cold sheets.

I would apologize to her and win her back. No matter what it took because I loved her.

27

ZAIN

"Why did you wake us up so early?" Zayed yawned, his hair all over the place as he entered the study wearing pajamas, with bananas all over them.

We all stared at him. Me, Khalid, Zara, Rahim and our grandmother. Only he was the one wearing pajamas, while all of us were dressed up, ready for the day.

"It's ten in the morning," Zara deadpanned.

"Is it?" He looked out of the balcony to see the sun and squinted his eyes. "Yes, it is."

"As I was saying before Zayed interrupted us. I want to bring Nasrin back and by the way I treated her, she is mad at me," I announced.

"She definitely hates you," Zara agreed, nodding her head. "Probably punch you when she sees you."

Everyone murmured their agreement while I gaped at them. "That doesn't help me."

"We are not here to tell you pretty lies, Zain. You fucked up and you are owning your mistake," Khalid said, and rolled out the map of Azmia and Maahnoor. Rahim helped him with pointing out the capitals and making a red circle where our palaces were situated.

My brother was right. Again. It was about time that I accept my mistake of pushing Nasrin away when I could have handled it way better. I didn't have to treat her as a sultan would, I should have listened to her and talk to her like her husband. Because of that, she had almost been killed with poison. I would never forgive myself if that had happened.

I will go to Maahnoor and bring her back.

"Sultan, allow me to arrange your safe journey to Maahnoor," Rahim said, already making a plan and writing it down.

"I will beat some sense into you before you leave," Khalid said, crossing his arms. I nodded at him.

Zara beamed, her smile giving me hope. "I can ask Nasrin to give you a chance so you can talk and make out and woo her back!"

"You are reading way too many romance books," Zayed commented and yelped when she pinched his arm.

"Thank you, Zara, that would be helpful."

"I will make sure the palace is ready to celebrate the return of Sultana," my grandmother piqued in, smiling at all of us.

We all agreed and started planning about my journey to Maahnoor and how I should talk to her without getting stabbed and win her back.

"Hey." Zayed frowned at all of us. "What should I do?"

"We almost forgot that you are useful to us," Khalid commented and glanced down at the map before looking at his friend. "Provide us with the fastest horses you have."

Zayed grinned, "On it!"

"But why horses?" I asked.

"Because horses make everything more romantic, duh!"

Zara answered, shaking her head as if it was common knowledge. *Maybe I should invest in romance books from now on.*

♔

"WHATEVER HAPPENS, DON'T GET KILLED." KHALID WISHED ME his good luck when I climbed the horses, making sure I had everything that I needed.

"You say that because you don't want to be crowned as the sultan," I teased.

He smiled, "You know me so well, Brother."

"Don't forget the gift!" Zara said when the guards started moving, the sound of their horses neighing surrounding us.

"I won't," I replied, and looked at the palace one last time. I hope I will have Nasrin riding with me when I see the palace again.

I couldn't risk having Khalid, Zara, or Zayed with me. Like how we travelled differently through airplanes to be safe in case something happens. I didn't want to risk their lives for a mistake that I had caused.

I hadn't told them about the risk of sneaking into the palace of Maahnoor. If I get caught by their guards, I would be as good as dead. The people of Maahnoor, especially the royal staff, were angry with Azmia for taking Hamid Elbaz as hostage. Even if he had been accused of murder, it was a crime to take a guest as a hostage. I had done just that by ordering him to be kept in the dungeons when he had visited Azmia to have lunch with us and his daughter.

That is why I have to try my best not to get caught. Or they would keep me as their hostage.

The sound of horses galloping was pressed down by the harsh wind of the night. Our plan was simple, go to the Palace of Maahnoor, talk to Nasrin, woo her with my charms and good looks and bring her back to Azmia where she belonged. Rahim had suggested to travel in the night and reach the palace before dawn. As Maahnoor was our neighboring country, the desert provided us with the access of sneaking into the country.

I could use a Jeep or a helicopter, but that would create noise and attention that we didn't need. If they caught me in Maahnoor with Nasrin, the council would think that I was a suspect in my own mother's death. Whatever happens, I have to try my best not to get caught. Or get killed.

Reaching the palace of Maahnoor was easy, sneaking inside it was easier. I made a note of reforming and restructuring the palace of Maahnoor after seeing the cracked walls and chipped paint. It barely stood a chance against an earthquake, and it pained me that I had allowed Nasrin to stay there thinking it was safe.

"Fancy seeing you here, Your Grace."

I turned, short knife in hand, and took a sharp breath when the barrel of the gun was pointed between my brows. I sighed, seeing who it was. "Elena. I didn't think you would be here."

She grinned and lowered the gun and tucked it safely in the band of her jeans. "How could I ignore you begging me for a favor to keep an eye on your wife? She is very cute by the way."

I smiled at her green eyes, her blonde hair tucked into a ponytail. I wished I had the time to greet an old friend, but I didn't. "Where is she?" I asked and like a professional she was, she led me straight to her room. Well, below it.

"Climb it. It will be easier to escape." Elena said, her eyes assessing the empty hallway and the barren gardens as I stood below the balcony of Nasrin's room.

"Why escape?" I asked, tucking the knife back into its sheath.

"Just a hunch. I will keep an eye out," she said, and winked at me. "Go get your girl, Zain."

Giving her a nod, I rubbed my palms and started climbing the wall, wincing when the edge of my fingers burned against the plaster. *Mental note: add more safety in the palace.* If I could easily breach it in a matter of minutes, then anyone could.

"What are you doing?"

I screamed. Nasrin screamed.

"*What the fu—*" I gasped and scrambled up on the balcony. I leaned against the railing and rubbed my chest where my heart thudded loudly. "You scared me."

She stared at me, her eyes wide. "I should be the one saying that! What are you even doing here? Climbing a wall? Are you hurt?"

"I am here to woo you and not get stabbed," I blurted. "No, I am not hurt."

Her eyes softened before they turned dark and she punched my jaw, almost pushing me down the railing of the balcony. I hissed and rubbed the small throbbing on my jaw.

"Okay, I deserved that," I said and blinked at her, watching her rub her red knuckles and murmuring something along the lines of 'fucking handsome face.'

"Nasrin, is everything okay?" Someone shouted from the doors of her room as I took in the plain white sheets and four-poster bed. No riches or opulence surrounded it. It was plain and boring... nothing like Nasrin. How could she live in a room like this?

"Yes, I... I saw a scrambling cockroach and punched it," Nasrin answered, glaring at me.

"You punched a cockroach?" The guard asked through the door.

"Yes, go away. I am okay." She turned towards me and pointed at me, "You."

"Me."

"*You.*"

"*Me.*"

"Why are you here?"

"Because I am sorry for being an asshole. I shouldn't have pushed you away and ordered you to stay here when I could have listened to you."

"Yes, you are an asshole," Nasrin nodded, crossing her arms, my eyes lowering to the tee shirt she wore. It was odd seeing her in such casual clothing. Shorts, tee shirt, and her bare feet. She looked young.

I licked my lips.

"*Wow,*" she scoffed, throwing her hands in the air. "You have the audacity of pushing me away, sneak up into my room at midnight and give me *that* look."

"What look?" I blinked at her innocently.

"The look that means you want to have teenage role-play sex with me!"

I blushed and eyed her bed. "Well, I was thinking about having sex with you in your childhood room."

Nasrin didn't reply because she was too busy eyeing me and the bed. I smirked, taking a step towards her but she shook her head. "No, I am still mad at you," she said stubbornly, keeping her chin high.

"I know." I took a step closer.

"Really mad, Zain," she whispered.

"Mm-hmm."

Another step.

"Like I want to stab you multiple times and leave you to rot in the desert mad."

I blinked down at her. "That's very expressive."

"I have thought about it a million times."

She was smiling.

Aw, God, she looks adorable.

"What else did you think about me?" I asked, breathing in the jasmine scent of her. *This is home.* "Did you think about the time when we were naked in the bath? That night in the pool? Or that time—"

"Yes. I hated myself for thinking about it because even though you treated me like that, I couldn't stop missing you." She forced her words out, looking away from me and stepping back.

"I am sorry, Nasrin. Stab me, if that's what you wish, but please give me another chance. I will do anything."

"Anything?"

I nodded.

She looked me in the eye and said, "Then kneel."

I dropped to my knees, looking up at her. "This is kind of sexy, not going to lie."

Her face turned red as she tucked her hair behind her ear. "Will they execute my father?"

My smile dropped. I nodded.

She took a sharp breath and rubbed her arms. "What about my brothers?"

"Council will question them, but not as... strictly like your father, because he confessed that no one from your family knew what he had done. I am trying to push them hard enough so they won't question any of you and sympathize with you."

"Okay. Thank you."

"Nasrin?"

She glanced at me, still on my knees in front of her. I handed her the small bottle of the custom-made perfume as she frowned at it, taking a small sniff.

She grinned. "This smells like jasmine!"

"It does. It's for you."

"Why me?"

Stupid fool.

"Because I love you."

Nasrin almost dropped the bottle and gaped at me. I continued, "I love you and I am sorry that it took me so long to realize. I-I wanted to let you know how I feel about you. You don't have to say it back, of course. Only when you are ready and comfortable."

She parted her lips and shook her head as if she was surprised. "Zain, I… I don't know w—"

"Nasrin, open this door now!" The guards yelled and her doors shook. I heard Elena's soft whistle of warning and I knew my presence was known to the guards of Maahnoor.

"You have to leave, now!" Nasrin helped me up and took me to the balcony.

"Is that it?" I asked, my voice small. "I can't leave. I want to spend more time with you. Come with me, Nasrin. You don't have to return my feelings, but come with me. Let me keep you safe. Please, come to Azmia."

The guards yelling got louder, and I knew I had to leave if I wanted to get out alive. But I couldn't move. I had promised myself that I would bring Nasrin back with me. No matter what happened.

"Zain," she whispered my name as if it was the answer I needed.

I understood. My promise to myself didn't matter because she didn't want to come with me. It was her choice.

"It's okay," I lied and forced a smile as I stepped back and dived off the balcony with the help of a wall when the guards broke the door.

28

NASRIN

"It's okay," Zain lied as his eyes met mine briefly before he dived, my heart lurching in my throat at the sight of him falling down. I glanced down, watching him run in the empty hallway and turned back, hiding the bottle of the perfume when guards stormed in my room.

I couldn't believe that he was here. His scent of cologne lingered in the air. I answered numbly to the guards, pointing towards the gardens when they asked me where the Sultan of Azmia was hiding.

Please be safe.

Zain was here, and he had confessed that he loved me. *I love you.* I never knew such a sweet sound existed until I heard him whisper those words. He came all the way from Azmia to my room to sneak me away back to Azmia, and I hadn't even given him a proper reply before he left.

"They found him near the gates!" The guards shouted, making me snap my head at them.

Zain would be as good as dead if the guards of Maahnoor found him. They were angry with Azmia for taking my father as hostage when he came to visit me for lunch that day. They knew my father was wrong, but they considered it a crime to take a guest as a hostage. If my father was going to die, they would kill Zain too if—

No. I wouldn't let him die. I couldn't.

I followed the guards with a shawl wrapped around me. I couldn't believe the number of guards that were unconscious in the dim hallways. The stench of copper and sweat mingled in the air as I ran downstairs towards the gates, my eyes searching for my husband.

"Zain!" I yelled when I saw him fighting the guards of Maahnoor. His face was covered in dirt with a slash of blood on his cheek. The number of his guards was very small compared to our guards.

No, no, no.

"Nasrin, what are you doing here?" Sadiq commanded.

"Trying to stop this madness," I said, storming towards the gates, but he wrapped his hand around my arm, stopping me. "Let me go, Sadiq!"

"We are taking the Sultan of Azmia as hostage and will return him to his home if Azmia returns our father," Sadiq said, his eyes cold.

I laughed, trying to free myself from his hold. "Are you listening to yourself? Use your fucking head for once. Our father killed his mothers and Zain didn't plunge a sword through his chest when he confessed his crimes. He let the council decide our father's fate because he is a sultan. If you care about being a good leader, you will stop our guards and let him go, because he has never hurt us."

"I can't do that, Nasrin. You don't know what it takes to be a sul—"

"I am so tired of hearing your bullshit. Take some accountability before you ruin your country." I bit his arm. He hissed, dropping my hand as I ran towards the gates, waving through the sand that flew around, chaos and shouting surrounding me.

I found Zain struggling to fight when the angry guards kept pouncing on him. It was madness.

"Stop!" I shouted as loud as I could, weaving between the fighters and ducking until I pushed away the angry guards from Zain who breathed heavily, blood and cuts all over his body. "Stay back!"

"I am okay, Nasrin." Zain coughed.

"What are you doing?" Sadiq snarled, standing across me, ready to hold my hand and take me away from him but I smacked it away, glaring at him.

"Touch me again and I won't be held accountable for my actions," I threatened him. I heard Zain whisper, "so hot," as he wiped blood from his face, wincing.

"As the Sultana of Azmia and the Princess of Maahnoor, I order you to stand down. Zain Al Latif is my husband, and if you harm him, you are harming your own princess. If you do not want to be executed, leave."

Silence surrounded us, and even Sadiq looked nervous to say anything. When no one moved, I yelled, "Right now!"

They all scrambled back, whispering to each other when Sadiq stayed. Elena, the guard who had saved my life from the poisonous food, helped me hold Zain up. Even her hair was matted with blood and dirt, her suit jacket was missing and her white shirt looked crumpled with rips.

"You touch him, and I will stab you," I warned my older brother. "Multiple times."

"And here I thought blood is thicker than water," Imran drawled as he eyed Zain and me.

"I care about you, but I also care about my husband. Don't make me choose between the two, and help me clean him up."

They both grumbled but helped Zain into the palace,

Elena trailing beside me as Zain whined about not needing any help. I chuckled when Imran smacked his arm where Zain was hurt and watched him hold back a whimper.

"Thank you for helping me and Zain. It means a lot to me," I said to her. The guards who were fighting before helped my husband and the guards of Azmia, apologizing for their anger.

"No need to thank me, Nasrin. He is my friend and so are you." She grinned. "Plus, I love using my guns and knives. Helps me feel stable."

I chuckled awkwardly.

"So what now?" she asked, pointing at the stairs of the Court Room where Zain was pouting. Sadiq and Imran were teasing him by the grin on their faces and applying childish *Barbie* and *Hannah Montana* stickers on his boo-boos. Their words, not mine.

Men.

"We will have to leave for Azmia as soon as he is better and wait for what the council has to say."

"I didn't mean about that, Sultana. I meant about you two. I mean, you two were pretty cute on the balcony."

I blushed thinking about it. "I will go back with him, but it will take me some time to get used to my feelings for him."

Elena nodded. "Of course. It took me a lot of time to accept my hate for someone."

"Who?" I asked.

She chuckled darkly, "Let's pray I don't see his pretty face again." She pushed me towards Zain. "Go save him from your brothers. He looks like he needs your help."

He did, pouting at me and begging me with pleading eyes.

29

ZAIN

"God, I am so tired," Nasrin whined, stretching her limbs in the rumpled sheets of the bed.

I smiled proudly, pouring a glass of water for her. "Feeling better, wife?" I purred, trailing my hand towards her naked breast before she smacked it away.

"No. You have a stamina of a horse. Give me a breather, Zain." She winced when she sat up, looking down at her lap that was covered in thin sheets. "We have been locked inside this room for three days."

"And it's still not enough for me," I said, handing her the glass.

"Insatiable."

As soon as we returned to Azmia, we had a small celebratory dinner with our family where we went through the tale of my wife saving my ass. Everyone was happy except the council, but I could deal with them later. I was glad that even her brothers had accepted me as their own.

Since that dinner, I had announced to the guards not to knock at the door unless they wanted their arms cut off. So I had spent days, afternoons and night worshipping her body, making love to her, making up for the week we had been apart from each other.

Nasrin patted the space beside her and I joined her in the bed, her eyes trailing over my naked body, frowning at the small cuts that were healing. "Zain."

"Nasrin."

"We didn't use protection," she said slowly, twirling her finger on my collarbone.

"Because I don't mind the idea of having a baby with you. Or four," I said truthfully.

"Four babies?" She gaped. "What changed your mind?"

I rubbed the strand of her hair between my fingers. "I am afraid of living in the past and comparing myself to my father. My biggest fear was to turn out like him, and that's why I never took pleasure in anything. Friends, alcohol, or even sex. But you helped me enjoy little things, and I want to live and see what future holds with you. If we are lucky enough to have a child together, she or he would be more precious than anything for me."

She cupped my cheek. "Are you sure, Zain?"

I nodded, kissing her on the lips. "I am, but only if you are."

Nasrin gave me a small smile and pushed me down onto the bed, straddling me. I licked my lips at the bare sight of her breasts, her taut stomach covered in hickeys. I groaned when she gave a small hump, my semi-hardened member sliding across her wet folds.

"I am ready, Zain. More than ready," she whispered and kissed me, riding me slowly until warm sunlight swept in our room through the balcony.

I winced when the sound of utensils clanked with each other in the early morning, my feet light as I kept them on the vast island of the palace kitchen. I had to wake up before Zain to sneak out of the room to the kitchen. Knowing he was on our bed, naked and alone, with a pout on his lips when he slept made something tug at my heart.

I am doing this for him.

Without thinking too much, I got to work wearing the apron. After I had prepared the sugar syrup and the filling, I started working on the crust, knowing Zain would start looking for me in a few moments. I worked quickly, putting the sweets in the oven.

"What are you doing?"

I let out a surprised gasp and turned around to see Khalid frowning at me, standing near the door of the kitchen.

"You scared me," I said, lowering my hand from my thundering heart. "I was making something sweet for your brother. And the family."

"*Liar,*" he said with a smug smile. "You are only making it to impress my brother."

I didn't reply, twisting my fingers nervously.

"You don't need to do that. He worships the ground you walk on and can never shut up talking about you."

"Really?"

"Yes, really."

"Why is everyone awake so early?" Zayed said groggily, yawning as he walked in the kitchen. He was a close friend of Khalid and Zain, so it wasn't a surprise to see him at the palace. He was in the stables, in the study with Zain, in the art studio with Khalid, or teasing Zara.

"My sweet sister-in-law is making *kunafah* for my brother to impress him."

"Can I get some too?" Zayed asked, his bottom lip jutting out, "Please?"

I chuckled and looked at Zara when she trudged into the kitchen in her pyjamas, her short hair all over the place. "Whatever Zayed is having, I will have it, too. But more."

He flicked her forehead, and she punched him, which resulted in a morning duel between them while Khalid watched them with crossed arms, letting out a sigh.

I smiled at all of them and said, "I think I might like Zain."

"*Right*," Khalid drawled, a teasing glint in his eyes.

Zayed and Zara stopped wrestling to give me a look. "Of course, you like my brother, who doesn't?" Zara said.

"No, I meant," I look around, trying to express it. "That I more than just like him. That is why I woke up early to make him *kunafah*."

"Aw, that's really sweet, Nasrin."

"Will I get a piece of *kunafah* or no?"

"So you love him."

I smiled at Zara, remembered to make *kunafah* for Zayed when he visits next time and froze hearing Khalid's words. He gave me a long look that made me shiver. His eyes were more intense than his brother's and seeing him look at me like he knew what I was feeling made me feel weird.

"I have never felt it before, so I wouldn't know," I confessed in a small voice, thinking about the night where Zain had confessed on his knees. I had wanted to say it to him, but I couldn't because I was confused.

Zara came up to me and gave me a side hug. "It is as simple as waking up early to make something sweet for someone that you care about."

"Is that how simple love is?" I asked, blinking at all of them.

Khalid gave me a smile. "Yes. You both care about each other even when you two have different opinions and fight in the study."

"We don't fight," I said. "We just… argue politely."

When they gave me an amused look, I huffed and muttered he was right. With a cloth, I pulled the hot tray of *kunafah* from the oven and let it cool down, smacking Zayed's palm when he tried to touch it.

"Well, love or not, you are definitely good for him. For Azmia and for our family," Zara said with her bright smile, a dimple on her cheek.

"Why is everyone in the kitchen?" Zain asked, looking at all of us and the *kunafah* cooling between us. "Is that *kuna—*"

"We just came to drink water," Khalid lied terribly and dragged Zayed out by his shirt when he said that he was there for *kunafah*. Zara gave me a thumbs up behind Zain's shoulder and closed the kitchen door, leaving me alone with Zain. And the delicious *kunafah*.

He frowned at the door. "What were they doing here?"

"Talking. We all were talking," I said. "Sit, I made this for you."

"For me? So early in the morning?" Zain asked, eyeing the

kunafah when I cut it, the cheese stretching out when I served a slice to him on a plate.

"Go on, eat it," I pressed when he eyed the plate and me.

He finally did. I grinned when his eyes went wide at the taste and he took another bite. "This is delicious. The best *kunafah* I have ever had, Nasrin."

Zain pulled me on his lap, feeding me a bite and making me promise to make the delicious sweet every week. I chuckled at him and gave him my promise.

"Zain," I said, cupping his jaw. "I want to tell you something."

He allowed me to continue, his hands resting on my waist, watching my lips when I licked them.

"I have been thinking about it for a while and realized that... that I..."

"Go on, Nasrin. Tell me."

"ThatIloveyou."

"What? I couldn't hear you."

I took a deep breath and said, "That I love you, Zain."

Zain stared at me, his pupils dilating. Cupping my cheeks, he said, "Say that again, Nasrin."

I blushed, smiling at my husband. "I love you, Zain."

He kissed me, and I kissed him back. Our kiss was sweet like *kunafah*. It was beautiful and... loving. We were smiling and murmuring 'I love you' when Zayed opened the door with a yell.

"My *kunafah*!"

We were so shocked with our confession and the sweet kiss that we didn't even blink when Zayed stole the sweet and ran out of the kitchen.

"Did Zayed steal my *kunafah*, or did I imagine it?" I asked Zain.

He rubbed my waist. "It really happened, Nasrin. Do you want me to fight to get it back for you?"

I shook my head. "It's okay. Can we go back to what we were doing before?"

He gave me a mischievous smile. "Of course, we can, my wife. Tell me how much you love me when I fuck you—"

"Zain!" I exclaimed when he laid me on the island. "Not in here."

"Fine. But I am not letting you out of the room until lunch."

"Such a bossy, Sultan."

I chuckled at him when he held my hand and ran with me to our room, ignoring the curious glances of guards and maids who saw their ruler and his wife running around the hallways of the palace like little children with huge grins on their faces.

THE END

READ EXPLICIT BONUS SCENE HERE
Or type this link into your browser:
https://mailchi.mp/cae223e541de/
bonussceneofdirtywildsultan

Thank you so much for reading Dirty Wild Sultan! If you enjoyed reading this book, I would be grateful if you could leave a review on the platform(s) of your choice.

Reviews help other readers like you find this book and are hugely appreciated by authors!

Love always,

Mahi

EPILOGUE

ZAIN

"Zain, I…" she moaned, her legs quivering with pleasure when I licked her soaking pussy.

"Shh, be quiet, Nasrin," I whispered, holding her thighs and standing up.

She looked at me over her shoulder, "It's your fault if we get caught."

I smiled and shook my head at my wife who was bent over the desk of my study, the expensive dress pulled over her waist. I lowered the zipper of my pants and said, "You are the one who told me you needed me inside you while we were greeting our guests. I just obliged the request of my beautiful sultana."

Her cheeks flamed hearing me and she pushed her hips back. "Yes, I need you inside me, Zain. Please, hurry."

"Try to be quiet," I said, wrapping my hand around her hair and sliding inside her warm heat in one slow thrust.

We both groaned at the pleasure of our union, her tight walls clenching my length tightly when I slowly fucked her. I pulled at her hair, kissing her lips when I slammed inside her, swallowing her moans as people mingled outside.

"Faster, Zain," she groaned, lowering her hand to rub herself.

I moaned into her skin, increasing my pace. I knew Nasrin was close when she squeezed her eyes shut, her body trembling when she reached her climax. I couldn't stop my orgasm when her walls spasmed around me, clamping me in a tight clutch when I released inside her.

Our breathy sighs echoed in the study. I gently pulled out from her, taking the tissues to clean myself up and help her when she stood up, her body swaying as I held her and asked if she was okay.

"I am," Nasrin said. "Maybe it's the postcoital bliss."

I chuckled and helped her zip up her dress while she fixed her hair that I had tugged and pulled during sex.

"Why did you call me Limerence when we first met?" Nasrin asked, watching me fix my shirt and zipping my pants.

"Have you seen Khalid's famous painting?" I asked, licking my lips. "He named it *Limerence* because he has been infatuated with someone. I never understood it until I saw you. Even in my drunken state, you looked so endearing to me, so carefree that I wanted to know you, cherish you."

Her pupils were dilated as she shook her head, wiping the corner of her eyes. My heart hammered in my ears, seeing her cry. Nasrin rarely cried. I didn't enjoy seeing her cry, or being the reason for those precious tears.

"You wreck me, Zain," she breathed, wrapping her arms around me. "That's what you said after our wedding night. You wreck me too, Zain."

I understood her, closing my arms around her and kissing her dark hair. We stayed like that for a few moments, holding each other.

After her confession, we both had talked about having children and stopped using protection. She had been working regularly at the vet clinic and with me while studying to make the laws of Maahnoor better. The council had taken Hamid Elbaz as a prisoner and announced her family not guilty. We didn't know why her father wasn't executed, but we didn't want to push our luck when they had ignored my breach in the Palace of Maahnoor.

We walked out of the study together and looked for my brother to wish him a happy birthday. It was Khalid's thirty-second birthday and as both Zara and Khalid were leaving Azmia, we had hosted a small party. Zara had worked hard to get into the same university as Khalid had once got his art degree from. She would learn photography and explore the world like she wanted to. Khalid was going to London for his upcoming exhibition of his paintings in one of their famous art galleries.

"What are you guys arguing about?" I asked Zara and Zayed when they bantered with each other while Khalid sipped on the glass of his wine.

"I was giving her sex ed," Zayed answered as my sister glared at him.

"I don't want to hear it. I already saw the horrendous presentation these two had shown me when I was eleven," Zara grumbled, looking at me and Khalid.

I protested, "It was not horrendous."

She deadpanned, "Khalid hand painted each sheet. No one does that!"

"Hey," Khalid frowned at her. "We did it for your knowledge."

"I know you did, but please tell Zayed to stop asking me if premature babies are made from precu—"

"Zayed!" I warned him, and Khalid smacked him on his head.

"Fine, I will go eat the *kunafah* Nasrin made," he grumbled, leaving the group clearly offended.

"Do you want to eat *kunafah*?" I asked my wife, who was rubbing her stomach.

She frowned at me. "No, I don't know why I don't like the taste of sweets anymore."

"You are kidding!" Zara gaped at her in horror.

"Yeah, I will go look for something sour," Nasrin mumbled, leaving her glass of wine untouched.

"I think she is pregnant," Khalid said casually, drinking the wine.

"You are not a doctor," I said, ignoring the tugging at my heart.

Maybe she was?

"No, but I am observant, unlike you," he shot back.

Zara said, "Maybe you should go after her. Apparently, the taste buds change when you get pregnant."

"How do you know about it?" Khalid narrowed his eyes at her.

"Because I read about it."

I ignored their pregnancy banter and went to look for my wife. I found her leaning against the pillar in the hallway, the glowing chandelier making shadows on her face, which was scrunched in pain.

"Nasrin, are you okay?"

My eyes widened when she puked, her hand clutching the pillar. I closed the distance between us and held her hair, soothingly rubbing her back.

Nasrin heaved, pulling back and taking my handkerchief to wipe her mouth when she said, "I never vomit."

"What do you mean?"

"That I never puke if I am sick, but I don't feel sick."

"Then…" I drawled, Khalid's words echoing in my head.

"I must be pregnant," she whispered at the same time, I said,

"You must be pregnant."

READ EXPLICIT BONUS SCENE HERE!

Want more of these filthy rulers?
Read Filthy Hot Prince Now!

UNKNOWN

The man in the black suit entered, locking the doors behind him. I eyed the scar on his forehead, leaning back on my chair and clenching my jaw.

"So?" I asked, trying to hide the anger in my voice.

He didn't dare to ask me to sit down, he knew I might reach for the blade and slit his throat. That's what I did to the last man I had sent for my mission, anyway. He had failed, and I needed to show them just how much *displeased* I was.

How they had failed me.

No one dares to do that.

"Someone from the guards caught the poison, Sir," he said, his deep voice turning into a stutter. "I-I don't know how but they are blaming the cook."

I exhaled sharply, closing my eyes. I didn't say anything for a few moments. The air thick and tense in the room.

"For now," I whispered, standing up and buttoning my suit.

"W-what?"

"They are blaming the cook for *now*, you shit." I glared at him. Grabbing his collar, I sneered, "This is why I told you to poison the water, not the food."

I pushed him back, pacing on the murky floor, my shiny shoes looking odd with it. "If you would have poisoned the water, she would be dead by now. Nasrin Al Latif would be dead and Zain wouldn't be able to do anything about it."

Raking my hand through my hair, I scrambled for my thoughts.

"What should we do now that... that the mission has failed?"

"Didn't one of you confirmed that Nasrin and Zain have been together since their marriage?"

"Yes, Sir. We even showed you the pictures."

Ah, right. The pictures of the royal couple in the heat of moment inside the study of Sultan of Azmia, Zain. They were creative with their... *positions*. I should give them that.

"*Hm*. We wait for now."

"But he is still weak—"

I pinned my eyes at him over my shoulder. "Zain Al Latif is not weak inside his goddamn Golden Palace. Nasrin is with him. So is his brother, the princess and that Sheikh Zayed. We cannot risk making a scene once more." I pinched the bridge of my nose. "We wait until they execute the cook. Send one of your cronies to get the job done and bring his tongue to me to make sure the cook is dead."

I looked at my reflection in the old mirror and smirked. "Nasrin Al Latif will get pregnant soon. We will strike then."

The man paled. "You don't mean to kill her when—"

"I. Do. *Not*. Care."

"I want to see Zain fall. I want to take away everything from him. Kill his wife, his child, his brother. Even his sister, Zara. She is a hot little thing, isn't she?" I chuckled, thinking about having her with me, holding her hostage and torturing her until Zain begs me to return her to him. I will be sure to send him her head once I am done with her.

"I want to see Azmia turn into ashes."

"This is not the right time because I want to paint you, Valeria," Khalid whispered in his deep, velvety voice.

"P-paint me?"

I could smell his musky scent when he crooned in my ear. "Yes. *Naked.*"

I trembled, my body reacting acutely to his teasing words.

He continued in his low voice, his finger trailing over my neck, "I want to paint your pale skin. Your neck. Your sensual body. Your stunning eyes. Your lush lips. Your red copper hair."

Khalid flicked my ear with his tongue, making me gasp when he whispered dirtily, "Your *tits.*"

"I can paint on you too, my sweet one." He planted a soft kiss below my ear. My breathing growing erratic and breasts aching to be touched. "Lay your naked body on my bed and paint on your bare skin with my hands. Would you like that, Valeria?"

I was clenching her legs tightly, melting hot desire gushing my underwear. My heart thudded loudly against my chest. I licked my lips and answered, "I… I would love that, Khalid."

EXCLUSIVE CONTENT

Want more exclusive content? You can sign up for Mahi's
Patreon to read steamy one shots every Saturday!

As a supporter, you get access to early drafts, exclusive VIP
content, deleted scenes, deleted chapters, cat pictures and
YOUR NAME in the Acknowledgements of my books.

www.patreon.com/mahimistry

PREVIEW OF TWISTED THERAPIST

IVY KNIGHT

"I am so sorry, Aiden, the traffic was so bad," I heaved, taking support of my knees to control my breathing. So much for dressing up in cute dress, applying light makeup and curling my hair in waves just for the session. I wiped down the sweat from forehead and straightened up, daring to peek at him.

Aiden looked like he always did. His face stern and no emotions showing on his face. His eyes travelled down my body and I held in my shiver when they raked over my bare legs.

He made a dramatic point of checking his wristwatch that cost more than the car that I drove and hummed. "We will talk about your tardiness after the session. *Sit.*"

I quickly sat down and drank some water, the breeze of the air conditioner cooling my skin. The session started, and we made usual talk about my day, what happened that week or if anything exciting happened that I wanted to share with him.

"How did your journaling go?"

We talked more about the days where I would write two-three pages a day or days when I could barely write a paragraph. He listened to me and asked questions when I would stop talking, urging me to drink water and keep going.

"Do you mind if I see what you've written?" He asked, his dark eyes soft.

My muscles tensed as I met his obsidian eyes. They ran over my body and noticed how stiff I had become. My eyes lingered on his crisp white shirt, stretching over his shoulders, the sleeves rolled up to his elbows with a dark-coloured tie. Maybe it was my imagination when I thought his eyes had stayed far too long on my chest and my legs. I shuffled in my seat and tucked the strand of my hair behind my ear.

Aiden's eyes flickered to my face, and he closed them for a moment, as if he was taking his time. He finally said, "You don't have to if you don't want me to read. I will understand and respect your privacy."

I licked my lips, trusting my instinct. "I-it's okay, I don't mind. You can read it."

I handed him the diary, frowning at the ruffled separate pages that I had shoved between them. He silently read the entry of my first day while I squirmed in my seat. I may or may not have drunk too much water, so I excused myself to the washroom.

When I came back, I could feel the change in the air. Aiden was sitting on the couch, but his posture was stiff. He barely addressed my presence when I sat down in my seat. I saw the diary was placed beside him and his jaw was clenched.

"Is everything okay?" I asked, my voice small.

He finally looked at me and the corner of his lips twitch. Leaning back on the couch, he said, "Yes, I suppose you could say that. I want to ask you something, Petal, and I want you to be honest about it."

Frowning, I nodded.

His eyes darkened, and he said in a stern voice, "Use your

mouth."

"I—*um*, yes, Dr. Aiden."

I didn't know why I *felt* the need to address him seriously.

"What were you doing this morning?"

My eyes widened, my heart pounding in my ears. I glanced at the diary and it struck me. Those ruffled pages. *Shit, shit, shit.* After journaling every day for a week, I wrote my fantasies regarding Aiden, my brother's best friend, on different torn pages. I always tucked them back in the diary, reminding myself to pull them out before I brought it to the session. But I was in such a hurry that I had completely forgotten about them.

Did he read it? I hope he didn't. I would rather eat raw broccoli than have him read all those pages.

Looking away from him, I lied and carelessly shrugged my shoulder, "I was meditating."

I mentally winced at my lie. He had tried coaching me to meditate, but I could never do it.

He is right. I am a terrible liar.

Aiden raised his eyebrows. "Is that so?"

I didn't like the tone of his voice. He seemed serious, and I prayed that the ground would swallow me up. He waited for my answer, crossing his arms over his chest. I got distracted by the way his biceps bulged, the veins on his forearms getting prominent.

He noticed me staring. I glanced down at my lap, twiddling my thumbs. "Y-yes, Dr Aiden, I was meditating and I-I focused on my breath like you taught me—"

"Why are you lying to me, Ivy?"

My head snapped at him. I shook my head, "I-I am not lying."

Aiden tilted his head and my throat went dry when he said, "Then why did I hear your voice moaning my name when you orgasmed with your fingers inside your pussy?"

PREVIEW OF DON'T DATE YOUR
BEST FRIEND

KIARA

"If you don't want to kiss me then . . . let's swim."

"Yeah, sure."

"Naked."

"*What?*"

"I always wanted to try skinny dipping." I pursed my lips and said, "And I really want to get out of these clothes."

When I thought about it, I wasn't feeling self-conscious about my body when it came to him. Yes, he had seen in me in bikinis and accidentally walking in when I was busy writing something on my Post-it in my underwear and bra. But I was never self-conscious about what he would think of me or my body. I did have stretch marks, but I wasn't uncomfortable about them. What I was most worried about was *myself*. If he got naked and my hormones spiked up, I didn't know if I would control myself and not jump on him.

Gosh, I sounded so bad in my head. Not to mention, my best friend would be the first guy I would ever see naked. *Way to go, Kiara.*

His voice was strained when he said, "What if someone catches *you* . . . me, both?"

I moved my damp hair over my shoulder. "We will be in the pool, Ethan. And no one can see us from the living room." I smirked when I said, "Unless you want to watch me while I swim, you can stay here."

The thought of Ethan watching me with his intense green-blue eyes while I was swimming naked in the pool sent a delicious shiver down my core.

His eyes darkened and he looked away, probably thinking the same when I noticed red blush creeping up his neck and making his ears and cheeks flush. *Cute.*

I prodded, "Come on, Ethan. Don't be a chicken . . ."

"*Fine.*"

He stood up, his tall frame towering me. I forgot how to breathe when his dark eyes seared me, slowly trailing down my body as if he had all the time in the world. His voice was rough when he said, "Remove that sweater first."

I raised my eyebrow at the sudden change in his demeanour.

Ethan said, "You have an extra piece of clothing than me."

I grinned. "Who said I was wearing any underwear?"

I loved the way his pupils widened in shock, surprise and then they were clouded by scorching desire. Biting my lips, I whispered, "I was messing with you."

Holding the hem of the sweater, I tugged it up and removed it. I straightened my damp hair and shivered. But it wasn't because of the cold air.

His eyes averted down my breasts, which were barely covered by the ivory lace bralette. As it was wet, he could easily notice my hardened nubs, which were begging for his attention.

We were crossing a dangerous line right now. And I knew neither one of us wanted to step back.

"Your turn," I managed to whisper.

ALSO BY MAHI MISTRY

Have you read them all?

Alluring Rulers of Azmia Series

Dirty Wild Sultan

Filthy Hot Prince

Tempting Rebel Princess

Charming Handsome Sheikh

Alluring Rulers of Azmia Complete Series Books 1-4

The Unfolding Duet

Don't Date Your Best Friend: Best Friends to Lovers

Don't Date Your Ex Best Friend: Second Chance Best Friends to Lovers

The Unfolding Duet Books 1-2

Dominating Desires Series

Twisted Therapist: Brother's Best Friend Age Gap Romance

Tempting Teacher: Student Teacher/Dad's Best Friend Age Gap Romance

Scan to easily access all of my books:

ACKNOWLEDGMENTS

Even though Zain or Nasrin's story is not a direct reflection of my own experiences, there were a few moments that I needed to write. I hope some of those moments will remind you that you are enough and you are loved.

I wish I could give *kunafah* to every reader. I am tremendously grateful for your kindness, generosity, and support. Thank you for taking time to read their story, it means the world to me.

To my wonderful family and adorable cats, thank you for making me dinner at eleven and for your unconditional love.

To my editor, Jeanie, thank you for your incredible hard work and pushing me to be a better writer. I can't begin to tell you how grateful I am to have you as my editor.

To all my wonderful friends, beta readers, proofreaders, arc readers, bloggers and book lovers, I couldn't have done this without you.

To all the wonderful Patreons who constantly support me with your sweet messages and uplifting comments.

Thank you to everyone who accepted the ARC edition of this book and helped me share this book with the world.

If you enjoyed reading this book, please don't forget to leave a review. I would really appreciate it. It helps find more readers like you and they are very important for authors!

ABOUT THE AUTHOR

Mahi Mistry has been writing since she was in middle school. Soon, she fell in love with writing passionate, steamy romances. Her stories have elements of humor, suspense and character development. Mahi's main purpose in her life is to make one person happy every day, even if that is a stranger reading her book and rooting for the main couple or her cats by giving them extra treats.

She enjoys simple things in life, like spending time with her family and friends, cuddling with her cats, reading and writing drool-worthy characters while sipping on hot chocolate from the wineglass to validate herself that she is actually an adult. She is an avid reader of fantasy, romance and thriller books and thinks writing about yourself in third person is atrocious. She firmly believes that cats rule the world.

www.mahimistry.com

9 789354 579097